ROOTS OF
Romance

Roots of Romance by Ania Whiteley

www.aniawhiteley.com

Text copyright © 2021 Whiteley Books Ltd
Cover artwork copyright © 2021 Whiteley Books Ltd
All rights reserved.

Published by Whiteley Books Ltd

This is a work of fiction. Names, characters, businesses, places, events, locales, and incidents are either the products of the author's imagination or used in a fictitious manner. Any resemblance to actual persons, living or dead, or actual events is purely coincidental.

All rights reserved. No portion of this book or it's cover may be reproduced, stored or transmitted in any form or by any means without the prior permission of the publisher.

First edition October 2023

Chapter 1

Given my incurable gardening addiction, getting side-tracked in Eden's Garden Centre was as inevitable as a weed in a rose bed.

Those damned petunias were my downfall this time. One moment, I was debating the subtle differences between the 'Purple Pirouette' and 'Rose Star' varieties, and the next, I was waving goodbye to the last taillights of the afternoon bus.

Typical.

As the first drops of rain descended and the last bus disappeared around the corner, I sighed loudly and wrapped my jacket tightly around me. I marched through Sagebourne, a little charming town in the middle of the Cotswolds, empty this time of this year save for a couple of locals. The rain started picking up, from a gentle drizzle to a steady pour. The cobblestone streets were quickly washed wet, the gutters filling with fast-moving streams, the atmosphere grey and dark. The evening was quickly creeping in.

I passed through the town and started walking down the country lanes. Trudging along, petunias cradled protectively against the rain, I let out a chuckle. Here I was, a professional gardener, at the mercy of the very nature I adored. It was like being at a party where you love the host but can't stand the guests. Only this time, the guests were the wind, the rain, and a seemingly endless country lane. I didn't even think about calling my parents to ask to pick me up: my dad was visiting his brother in a nearby town, and mum always went on a run at this time of the afternoon, regardless of the weather. Which has left me following the side of the road, thankful for not many cars around at this time of day.

The wind was already working up a tantrum, yanking at my hair and jacket like a mischievous sprite, and then, of course, there was the rain. Not a drizzle, not a sprinkle anymore, but a full-on, bucket-emptying, heaven-bawling downpour.

I just resigned myself to getting completely soaked because it would still take me thirty minutes to reach my parent's house, set on the outskirts of Sagebourne. Luckily, I walked the same road many times as a teenager, so at least I didn't have to worry about getting lost. I pressed my lips together, powering through, inevitably thinking that I didn't expect to be trekking down through these Cotswolds lanes again for a while. In the ideal world, I was back in London, my business thriving.

In fact, at twenty-three, I had no plans to be living long-term with my parents.

I mean, it didn't start as a long-term option. Once upon a time, in the golden age of post-university optimism, I pruned and planted for a living, helping Londoners maintain their gardens. My new gardening business was doing well enough to pay for my little studio flat and give me a comfortable lifestyle. I had so many plans in the pipeline: medicinal herbs workshops, gardening for kids, you name it.

I always found it funny: when my parents named me Jasmine, it wasn't because they explicitly expected me to be a gardener. I became one, nevertheless, if only for a year. Fond of my job and gardening metaphors, the world was my flowerbed, or so I liked to believe. I was the reigning queen of roses, the duchess of daffodils, and the baroness of, you guessed it, petunias. I honestly believed that my career would bloom into something amazing.

But then, as if out of a dystopian novel my dad was always so fond of, the lockdown hit. And even though the last lockdown was a year ago, my clientele vanished faster than a rabbit in a lettuce patch and never returned. Some of them moved out of the city, others, bored in lockdown, learned gardening skills and felt that they no longer needed me. Before I knew it, I couldn't afford my place in London. Before I knew it, I could hardly afford anything. Before I knew it, my flourishing career and life in London were as dead as an overwatered succulent.

It sounds dramatic, I know. But here I was, a young gardener trudging down a Cotswolds country lane, soaked to the bone, clutching my petunias, and mulling over my life choices. When my parents gently suggested I move back to my childhood home to live with them, I considered it an ultimate life failure. Still, the situation I found myself in left me very little choice.

To be fair, living with my parents wasn't that bad - I actually enjoyed it. The only problem was, it was meant to be a temporary solution, a month, max two. Three if we are pushing it. But six months in, there was no work, save for a couple of odd jobs for the locals. I was still in Sagebourne, pondering what to do next, relentlessly applying for jobs in bigger landscaping companies and continuously hitting the wall of rejections.

I still hoped for a place for myself, and it felt odd when my parents went to work, and I was left in the house, twiddling my thumbs. I hoped that now spring was on its way, more people would be interested in cultivating their gardens following a harsh winter. My career may have taken a detour, and my dreams may have hit a snag, but at least - I glanced at my petunias - I still had my plants.

That thought only cheered me up for a few seconds before I gave in to the temptation of checking my emails. It was Sunday, I knew. Still, it was a perfect enough day for someone to email me about some gardening work. I opened my inbox and sighed, seeing only an email about a discount from a candle company. Discount or not, there was no way I could afford to buy any candles soon.

Suddenly, a car came out from the corner; too focused on my phone I didn't notice it until a splash of cold water landed on my right side. I yelped, looking up just in time to see it speeding away.

"Oh, well, thanks for the shower, you absolute road hog!" I muttered to the retreating car, my voice drowned out by the steady fall of rain.

Before I could step forward, my foot slipped in the mud that I also hadn't noticed, too distracted by the car and my phone. With a spectacular lack of grace, I landed butt-first into the squelching mud.

"Oh, terrific!" I grumbled, trying to sit up and only succeeding in smearing more mud on my rain-soaked jeans. "And here I was, thinking today couldn't possibly get any worse," I muttered, looking at my ruined clothing.

It was then I remembered the petunias that fell from my hands when I tried to regain my balance. When I reached the flowers which rolled down towards the field, I was devastated to see their little heads were mostly broken. I gritted my teeth, hoping it would prevent tears from falling.

At that very moment, a yearning to be safely tucked in a busy London pub, enjoying pints with my friends, was overwhelming.

In the corner of my eye, I noticed that the car - a red Porsche, because of course it would be a red Porsche that sent me into the ditch and broke my flowers - stopped nearby, and a man jumped out. He was now marching towards me.

I wondered how annoyed I should be at him. To be fair, it was mostly my fault - I shouldn't have looked at my phone. But he also should have been more careful and not driven so fast. "Are you okay?" The man asked as soon as he reached my side. I could barely hear him; the rain was muffling any other noise. He wore relaxed binge chinos that looked out of place in this weather and what looked like an expensive waterproof jacket. I couldn't see his face much, hidden by a hood, but he looked around my age, maybe a few years older.

"I think so, yes," I grumbled, rubbing my shoulder. I glanced pointedly at what was left of my petunias.

"Oh no, your flowers… Shit, I am so sorry. I shouldn't have been driving so fast. I am honestly so sorry." He did, surprisingly, sound apologetic and worried. "Is your arm okay?"

"All okay, no harm done." I softened my voice.

"The flowers would disagree," he looked at the broken petunias. "Do you live around here?"

"Just at the end of this road," I explained.

"Why don't I drive you back home? That's the least I can do after nearly driving you over and ruining your plant."

Now, my best friend Caro would most certainly have said yes if a mysterious hooded stranger in a red Porsche offered her a ride home, but I was always the cautious one.

"It's okay, my house is not that far now. I will be fine. Thanks for stopping and checking on me, though. I appreciate it."

"Are you sure?"

"Yes. Thank you."

The man nodded. But he didn't move. "Wait," I sensed him carefully scanning my face. "*Jas Ackerley?*"

My jaw nearly dropped. There was only one person in my entire life who has ever called me Jas.

"Jasper Thornvale!"

Chapter 2

Why on earth was Jasper Thornvale here?!

A split second later, I discarded this question onto a pile called Stupid-and-Rhetorical. Naturally, he would be here; he lived on the outskirts of Sagebourne, just like my parents'.

My next question fell into the category of more appropriate ones: what do you actually say to your childhood friend and a teenage crush after not speaking to him for *years*?

"This is exciting!" he grinned. "Minus the part of me nearly running you over, of course," he gave me another apologetic look. "Come on in. I'll drive you back to your parents - I assume you are staying at theirs?"

Too stunned to speak, I nodded. As it was the most natural thing to do, Jasper reached out and placed his arm around me, scooping both me and my broken petunias and leading me towards his Porsche. I scrambled into the car with ridiculously low seats, and embarrassed, noted the state of my muddy jeans.

"Don't worry about it," Jasper noticed me looking. "It needs to be cleaned, anyway."

It was the shiniest car I have ever seen and inside and outside, it definitely didn't look like it needed a clean, so I appreciated him trying to ease my discomfort. We closed the door, and Jasper started the engine, warming the car up. He pushed his hood down, and it was strange to see he hadn't changed much: he was still tanned (used to be from all the running outdoors; now I imagined it was due to endless holidays), his eyes were still bright blue (which of course they would be, I scolded myself, wondering if the rain washed away the last of my brain cells), and his golden hair still left longer, so it curled behind his ears. It was only his jaw that became more pronounced and masculine, and even through the anorak, I could see he was no longer that lanky boy, instead putting on some muscles.

I had a crush on him as a teenager, and I was horrified to realise I could easily have a crush on him right now, too. But there was no way this was happening: I needed a job, and my own place and romance was literally at the bottom of my priority list.

As I opened my mouth to speak, the rhythm of the raindrops tapping against the car's roof suddenly escalated into a barrage.

A hailstorm. Tiny, icy pellets bombarded the car like millions of drumsticks hitting a cymbal. The sound was deafening, the noise echoing inside the confined space.

"I don't think I should be driving," Jasper pointed out. "Let's wait it out."

I nodded, "At least we're inside."

"Quite. Gosh, Jas, it's been ages," Jasper raked his hair, wet at the ends. "How are you doing?"

"Still no one ever calls me Jas," I smiled.

"Good to know I remain the chosen one," Jasper laughed, the soothing sound reminding me of honey. I took a deep breath. *No thinking about Jasper's soothing voice*, I scolded myself.

Instead, I thought I had always loved my name: with my white - blonde hair that I got after my mum's Scandinavian side and green eyes, I felt it suited me well, reminiscent of soft white jasmine flowers on the green vines. So, since I was little, I kept telling everyone to call me Jasmine, and none of the other shortened options would do. It was only when Jasper started to call us Jas and Jas that I allowed this small exception to the rule. As a child, I used to play a lot with Jasper's younger sister, Sienna, who was my age - but where Sienna preferred playing with dolls, Jasper was always up for adventures that involved pirates and superheroes and climbing trees, which I loved far more than dolls. I followed him around with a mixture of disgust and awe (he was a boy, after all).

But then Sienna went to boarding school and made different friends; our childhood friendship took its natural course, and year by year, we spoke less and less until we stopped altogether. Still, I would see Jasper around Sagebourne sometimes, and (I am embarrassed to admit) I have joined the ranks of teenage girls who practised their signatures as Mrs Thornvale.

I glanced at his hands, now relaxed on the steering wheel. No wedding ring.

"I have been running a gardening business, which has been really fun," I finally spoke.

"That sounds great! You have always loved running around our garden, so I can't say I am surprised," he smiled at me, and I smiled back, the memories of us escaping from imaginary trolls hidden in the garden's labyrinth flooding me with sudden warmth.

"Good times," I slowly relaxed into the comfortable seat.

"Sienna would disagree; you were her best friend, and you always preferred playing outside than with her dolls."

"True," I chuckled. "How is she now?"

"Really good. Climbing the ranks in the top law firm in London."

"London! I should definitely message her for a coffee."

"More like a midnight drink. She is that busy," he scoffed, but I could see he was proud of her. "Shame that we all lost touch."

"We should definitely organise a reunion," I suggested.

"I am all up for it," Jasper grinned, and my heart sped out, stupidly excited about the prospect of rekindling my friendship with Jasper.

Friendship, Jasmine. Just friendship. Nothing more.

"And how have you been?" I asked softly. I heard about his dad's death. But Jasper didn't mention it, instead telling me about just returning from Ibiza - he was there for a friend's wedding, but was about to get busy opening a new art gallery in Rome that he has recently invested in.

"So yes, a lot of travelling, but I love it; better Ibiza than old Blighty," he chuckled and glanced at the road ahead. The hailstorm stopped, leaving only a drizzle in its wake, and a part of me was… disappointed. It was strange how quickly I relaxed and how nice it was to sit with Jasper in his car, the world raging outside, and all we did was reconnect. It felt so easy, too, as if we never really stopped talking. Perhaps that's what I have always liked about him: he was just easy-going and fun.

"Let's attempt to get you home safely," he gripped the steering wheel.

"Let's please make it a successful attempt. My parents are probably worried by now." I let him concentrate on a particularly narrow corner before asking: "Are you planning to stay at Sagebourne for a while then, or are you back in Rome soon?"

"Ideally, staying until the gallery opens in August, and maybe going back for a week. So far, things have been going well, and I have a good manager, so hopefully, I can stay for a bit longer. I have a few weddings to attend as well in April and May."

"Anyone I know?"

"I don't think so; most importantly, they are not *my* weddings." He laughed.

"Still a commitment-phobe, aren't we, Jas?" I teased.

"Always," he nodded enthusiastically.

"Bet the drive to your house is littered with broken hearts."

"Then I am glad I am staying at my mate's," he laughed again.

"Is your mum in Sagebourne?" I asked, remembering I heard that these days she spent most of her time in the south of France.

"No," he answered, and despite a soft smile, I saw his shoulders tensing. I wasn't sure what to say, but as we pulled onto my parents' front drive, their charming red brick house appeared in the view and saved me from continuing with the subject. "Anyway, here we are. We should go out for a coffee and catch up properly… Jas. I am holding you onto that promise of reunion," he grinned at me.

"We should, Jas," I smiled back.

And then, a silhouette dressed in a bright pink jacket materialised outside my window, flapping their hands.

Arlene Ackerley, aka Mum, stood outside the car, peering inside. I quickly got out.

"Jasmine!" My mum exhaled a sigh of relief. "I have called you and called you!"

The one slight problem about living with my parents - it didn't matter that I was an adult now. They still worried when I didn't come home at the promised time.

"I am very sorry, Mrs Ackerley, this is entirely my fault. I nearly…"

"He just made me awfully wet, that's all," I interrupted before he could terrify my mother with a tale of my near-death experience.

But the ringing silence, Jasper's suppressed laugh and my mother's wide eyes made me choke back on my words.

"Jasper Thornvale!" My mum blinked a few times, cleared her throat and beamed at him. "How lovely to see you!"

"Pleasure to see you too."

"I didn't know you were around?"

"Ah, yes. I thought I ought to be home more often."

"Wise words. I must say it has been lovely to have Jasmine with us. She has been…"

"Mum, aren't we supposed to FaceTime Uncle Peter?" I interrupted her. I was cold, miserable, and after hearing about Jasper's ventures in Rome, I didn't necessarily want to reveal I was unemployed and living with my parents. I hoped that by the time we got to organise our reunion, I would be back in business.

"Why would we? Your father has literally just gone to see him," Mum gave me an utterly confused look.

"Don't let me hold you up," Jasper said politely, his hand on the car door.

"Nonsense! I tell you what, young man, why don't you come over for a tea? It's wicked weather out here; you both look absolutely drenched! Only a cup of tea would do!"

"Mum," I hissed at her, but my mother clearly joined the Jasper Thornvale Crush Club because she paid me no attention, staring at him instead with a suspiciously adoring gaze.

"Actually, that would be lovely," Jasper smiled.

"Wonderful!" Mum exclaimed and ushered us inside.

Wonderful indeed, I thought with a resigned sigh and followed her inside.

Chapter 3

A few minutes in there I was, in the familiar kitchen setting, nursing a cup of Earl Grey and trying to look as nonchalant as humanly possible after changing from my muddy clothes into something more dry and less dirty. To my right, Mum busied herself with the biscuit tin, and Jasper made himself comfortable across the table. He took his jacket off, and I couldn't help but smile: a knitted sweater. I wondered if this one was made by his mum, whom I remembered as obsessed with knitting jumpers and incredibly good at it. Just the sight of him in that jumper brought back an avalanche of memories – from climbing trees and fighting over who would be the captain of the ship when we were younger to awkward glances, unsent love notes, and one unfortunate incident involving a tampered locker and a rogue frog during my teenage years.

Those parts I would rather not remember.

"So, Jasper," I began, my eyes darting between my unsuspecting childhood crush and my well-meaning but overly honest mother. "How's the family?"

Before Jasper could respond, Mum jumped in. "Oh, I've heard they're all doing marvellously. His cousin just had a baby, you know."

"Ah yes, she did," Jasper smiled. "A healthy little boy. I am actually going to see them next week."

I shot her a glance, "Yes, Mum. I know. You've told me, remember?"

Turning to Jasper, she continued, ignoring my feeble attempt at damage control. "Jasmine here has always wanted a baby. Isn't that right, dear?"

Choking on my tea, I shot her a wide-eyed, 'For-the-love-of-all-that-is-holy-stop-talking' look.

"Actually, Mum, I think you're confusing me with-"

"Oh, and did I mention," she interrupted me, beaming at Jasper, "our Jasmine here is currently... exploring her options, which is just super exciting."

I groaned inwardly. 'Exploring her options' was mum-speak for 'jobless and living with her parents.'

"Really? That sounds fascinating," Jasper said, eyeing me curiously. There was a twinkle of amusement in his bright blue eyes. "You mean about your gardening business?"

"What Mum means is…" I desperately tried to intervene, only to be cut off once again.

"Yes, she's taking some time to figure things out," Mum declared, collapsing onto a chair between Jasper and me. "Which, of course, living at home really gives her the space to do that. David and I are really happy to have her here."

"Mum!" I almost shrieked, mortified. She sounded sincere and actually looked happy, which was lovely, but honestly, did she have to mention I am staying with them for a while?

Jasper, to his credit, chuckled. "Well, I think why not. I thought I ought to be home more often. Gives you time to...figure things out. A space to think, which to be fair, is a rarity in this busy world."

Mum nodded, her eyes shining with pride. "Exactly! The gardening business was going so well, and I am sure things will take off again. Our Jasmine here is like a seed, just waiting to sprout, you know? Right here, under our roof."

My face burned as I managed a strained smile, making a mental note to take Mum aside later for a crash course on the fine art of discretion. Meanwhile, I strongly suspected that the rest of the afternoon would be filled with many more cringe-worthy 'seeds waiting to sprout' moments.

"I think it's nice you are living with your parents," Jasper said, still smiling.

"It's temporary," I assured him quickly. "Just until... things get back to normal."

"Oh, normal is overrated anyway," Mum piped in. "You should see her room! It's turned into a veritable indoor garden. At this rate, we'll have our very own Eden Garden Centre upstairs."

I rolled my eyes, hoping Jasper would find this amusing rather than pathetic.

Not that I cared. As in… okay, I cared what he thought about me, but only because you don't want to meet your childhood friend as an adult only to tell them you are struggling.

"Actually, I love gardening," Jasper said, surprising us both. "I've been trying to get a few things growing on my balcony in my flat in Rome."

That was it. My moment. An opportunity to save face and talk about something I was good at. I launched into a passionate speech about the therapeutic benefits of gardening, how it's so much more than just a hobby, almost like a way of life.

"The ideal pH for azaleas, you see," I continued, determined to finish the story about my latest project for a wealthy London family, "is slightly acidic, around 4.5 to 6.0. Azaleas are acid-loving plants and-"

While I was midway through my speech, a thoughtful expression appeared on Jasper's face. He listened intently, his eyes flickering with a spark of interest I hadn't expected.

Maybe I was yet to save this disastrous conversation.

"Jasmine, that sounds really impressive," Jasper said, and although I searched for a hint of mockery in his voice, I found none. "And you have mentioned you are in between the jobs. That sounds like you might have some availability in the summer?"

My ears pricked. "I guess I do? I mean, I do. I definitely do."

"You probably remember my house, right?" I nodded: calling it just a house was a bit of an overstatement. Thornvale Manor was a grand stately home, full of corridors and bedrooms and with a vast amount of land. "Since my father passed and Mum moved to live in the south of France, the garden fell into disarray. It's basically overgrown, wild, and generally pretty neglected. Seeing it like this is sad, given how much my parents loved it…" Jasper cleared his throat. "Anyway, I would love to bring it back to life, but I need professional help. How would you feel about helping me to restore it? I would employ you, of course - we could sign an initial contract from June to August, with a start date being the 1st of June, what do you think? I am also renovating the old cottage on the grounds at the moment, and you could live there. The renovation is planned to be finished by the end of May and might be easier than commuting daily. What do you think?"

"Well, Jasmine dear," Mum chimed in, sipping her tea, "this sounds like a splendid opportunity. It's not every day one gets to restore a grand manor garden, right?"

I shot her a glare that clearly said, 'Not helping, Mum.' But there was no denying the sudden rush of excitement at Jasper's offer. Initially, I bristled, feeling that he was taking pity on me. But it was clear his parents' love for the garden was important to him, and after he mentioned renovating the cottage, it sounded like he was genuine about breathing some life into the neglected parts of the estate.

"You'd really trust me with that?" I asked, trying to keep my voice steady.

"I can't think of anyone better," he said sincerely.

I blinked in disbelief. That was it. My chance to do what I loved and perhaps impress my teenage crush in the process. I have never worked on a garden as big as the one belonging to the Thornvales - it would look brilliant on my portfolio.

All in all, the day was turning out much better than I could have ever anticipated, despite Jasper nearly running me over. And thankfully Mum hadn't blurted out anything about my penchant for singing to my plants – that would probably make Jasper think twice about his offer of employment.

"I would love to accept your offer, Jasper Thornvale."

His blue eyes locked with mine. "Then it's settled."

"R-really?"

"Yes. I probably have to dash off now. I am staying at my mate's and promised him a gaming session, and it's getting late, but hey, listen - I am going to send through all the details later in the week. Any questions, just let me know. Is that okay?"

"Sure. Sure," I hopped off the chair and walked him to the door. "That sounds great."

"Is there anything else you'd need from me besides the normal employment contract stuff?"

"Anything to do with how the garden used to look like: old photographs, old plans, anything like that would be useful."

"Great. Consider it done." He smiled. "I am excited for you to start."

"Me too." I pushed my chin up, looking at his sparkling blue eyes, my heart hammering against my chest.

"And it would be nice to have another summer together," he added with a mischievous smile before opening the door and letting in the cold air that thankfully cooled my flushed cheeks. "See you later, Jas."

"Drive safely!" I waved at him, watching him disappear inside his car. As the engine revved and the red Porsche drove off, I closed the door and re-joined Mum in the kitchen.

"Have I just got a job?" I collapsed onto a chair, reaching for a glass of white wine Mum swiftly produced from the fridge.

"You did! So exciting! Cheers!" We clink our glasses, and she sat beside me. "And at the Thornvale Manor of all places! It would look so good on your portfolio."

"It really would," I grinned. "I honestly thought today would be written off, and then… I got a job."

"The day was clearly not over yet. And Jasper is such a lovely boy. I am sure you would work great together. He seemed really passionate about that garden." Mum took a sip of wine and frowned suddenly. "Oh, golly. Was I talking too much? I was talking too much, wasn't I." She looked pretty mortified.

I sighed loudly and placed my hand over her shoulder. "Understatement of the century."

"But I am just genuinely excited to have you home!"

"That's precisely the problem, Mum." I groaned.

"Alright, I shall just drink and say nothing," she made a gesture of zipping up her lips and throwing away the key.

"Probably for the best," I giggled, pulling her closer.

Chapter 4

Even when the first of June finally arrived, I still could hardly believe my luck with Jasper's offer. I signed the contract, and last week, Jasper sent a final email confirming my start date. We emailed back and forth with the plans for the garden, and even when I researched Jacobean manor gardens, I still expected him to withdraw his offer at any time. I struggled to believe my luck.

So it was only when my parents dropped me off in the afternoon of a particularly warm Sunday at the beginning of June that the reality finally sunk in.

Jasmine Ackerley, a head gardener (okay, the *only* gardener, but still) in Thornvale Manor.

I stepped out of the car just before the impressive iron gates of Thornvale Estate that were left ajar. I grabbed my suitcase and said goodbye to my parents, promising to meet them next weekend for dinner in Sagebourne so I could update them on my first days at work. As their car disappeared back into the main road and I stepped through the gate, I drew in fresh air and took a moment to appreciate the scene before me.

The driveway stretched out, an elegant charcoal ribbon woven through an emerald expanse of lush trees. Sunlight streamed down through their leafy canopies, creating patterns of light and shadow on the ground beneath. A cool breeze rustled through the foliage, carrying the scent of damp earth and fresh greenery. I remembered it to be impressive as a child, and as an adult, it was impressive still.

As I walked, the crunch of gravel beneath my boots and the suitcases echoed through the silent expanse, the only sound apart from the occasional chirp of a hidden bird. The trees thinned as I neared the heart of the estate, gradually revealing the manor house.

There it stood, a majestic building nestled amongst the trees, an architectural testament to a bygone era. Tall, ivy-covered stone walls crowned by a slate roof glistened under the afternoon sun. Mullioned windows peered out. The manor was at once imposing and inviting; I was both intimidated by its past grandeur and enchanted by its future promise.

And then, I caught my first glimpse of the garden. I vaguely remembered it to be behind the house, but its tendrils stretched around it now as if the garden tried to embrace or forcefully claim the manor. Already, I could see the brambles tangled with wild roses, and the lawns were a patchwork of long grass and wildflowers, a palette of vibrant greens and yellows speckled with reds and blues. The doors to the main entrance's door were nearly completely covered by willowy white wisteria. I made a mental note it had to be cut, but I couldn't deny it had a certain charm. The only plants that strangely appeared to be in shape were the white hydrangeas stretching across the front of the manor house.

My phone buzzed furiously: my parents wished me good luck, and Caro was desperate for updates. She couldn't get over how much my improved job situation was like something straight out of the rom-coms that I loved to read: a poor gardener employed by a handsome lord of the manor and a summer full of hot sex.

I scoffed at that and firmly told Caro I had to focus on the job, only secretly hoping the latter would be on the cards. Jasper wanted to meet with me after we shook hands on my new role in my parent's kitchen, but problems with his art gallery called him back and forth to Rome. He was back in England last week when he sent me his email and signed it saying he was looking forward to spending summer with me.

From which I deduced that hot sex could be on the cards. This wasn't a bad thought, especially given that sex had never been on my cards. Or rather, it had been, but I never felt I'd found the right man - I dated a few guys at university, but what little romantic encounters I had, none of them felt even remotely close to any of the hot sex I read in my novels. And then, of course, lockdown was not conducive to any romance. I sighed and put down my suitcases, unsure what to do next and where to go.

Thankfully, from behind the manor, a woman trotted towards me. I carefully arranged my features into a polite smile that I hoped had nothing to do with me thinking about hot sex with Jasper Thornvale.

Her face lit up when she saw me.

"You must be Miss Ackerley!" A deep frown quickly replaced the woman's smile as she glanced at my suitcases. "Goodness, don't tell me you have dragged these heavy things all by yourself… Where the heck is Parker?"

"Oh, it's all good," I reassured her, recalling Jasper's email explaining that Parker was the family's butler, who was told to wait for me by the gates. "And please call me Jasmine. You must be Mrs Butterworth?"

"The housekeeper to the family, yes." She nodded proudly, and I vaguely recognised her from my childhood years. "I trust you had a good journey? Young master Jasper mentioned your parents live nearby?"

"They do. They live on the other side of Sagebourne. The journey was all good, actually. We went through the town to avoid the Sunday motorway traffic."

"Very wise," Mrs Butteroworth agreed. "I remember you from running around with young mistress Sienna. You two were always up for some mischief," she chuckled, her hazel eyes full of warmth.

Before I could reassure her that I was all professional now and definitely up to no mischief (unless it involved Jasper), Mrs Butterworth spun around, crossing her arms across her chest.

"Ah, there is Parker! Parker, honestly, you truly had one job-."

"I was looking for Buttons!" exclaimed the man who appeared from the other side of the manor. He was burly, with a red face and red moustache, and a huge frown on his forehead. "Rogue thing, escaped again!"

"Is Buttons… a goat?" I have no idea why I thought Buttons was a goat, but it seemed a reasonable assumption. Or a sheep. I imagined a goat happily running around, and I had to suppress a laugh.

"A goat?!" Roared Parker, utterly confused by my comment. "It's a bloody cat!"

Mrs Butterworth tried to keep her face at an appropriate state of annoyance, but even she seemed to fight hard not to laugh.

"Buttons is a family cat," she explained.

"A demon, rather!" huffed Parker.

"And with the Thornvale children being out of the house so often, Parker is responsible for the cat's wellbeing-,"

"They should have given it away, bloody nuisance, not a cat!"

"- but it has a knack for disappearing." Mrs Butterworth sighed and gave Parker a sideways glance. "But Buttons is very friendly and likes cuddles, should you come across him."

"You will never come across him, this infuriating creature!" Parker hollered and finally appeared to give up on his search for the infernal cat after looking around one more time. "Sorry, miss," he finally grabbed my suitcase. "But that bloody thing is doing my head in!" This earned him another stern look from Mrs Butterworth. "A'right, I will take your suitcases to the cottage right away. Oh, and welcome to the Thornvale Manor," he said and although he didn't smile, his features visibly relaxed.

"Thank you, Mr Parker."

"Just Parker," he marched towards the right of the manor, still cursing the cat under his breath, leaving me behind. I glanced at the housekeeper, unsure whether I should follow him.

"Honestly," Mrs Butterworth shook her head. "Parker ought to know better. The cat, I am sure, will appear shortly. It's a cat, for goodness sake, it's bound to roam around."

"Do you both live in the manor?"

"Yes," Mrs Butterworth smiled. "But it's only us. There used to be more live-in staff, but…" she paused and sighed. "Anyway, yes, for the moment, it's just us. There is a cleaning team that comes over every Tuesday and Friday, and we also have a food delivery coming on Fridays. I am sure young master Jasper explained that you are most welcome to eat in the manor, but the cottage has its own kitchen if you find that easier. You can also do both - just let me know if you would like to join us for breakfast or dinner."

"Yes, he did explain. And yes, that sounds brilliant; I will probably cook myself but wouldn't mind joining for an occasional meal."

"Brilliant, then it's settled. How exciting to have you here; I was delighted when young master Jasper spoke about restoring the garden. It really grew neglected. Master Eddie and Mistress Margot loved it very much," her eyes glazed as she looked at the manor. I knew she meant Jasper's parents. How sad it must have been to lose first Eddie Thornvale to cancer and then his wife, who couldn't live in the manor afterwards, broken by her husband's death. Mrs Butterworth must have been close to both - to lose them like that was cruel.

After a minute, Mrs Butterworth tore her eyes away from the manor house and looked at me with a soft smile. "Now shall we follow Parker? Best to make sure he delivers your suitcases, lest he goes on another hunt after Buttons, and this time, both the cat and the suitcases will go missing."

Chapter 5

We promptly went after Parker, turning around towards the manor's east side.

"Ah, there it is: the cottage you will be staying in. Young master Jasper had it freshly renovated." Mrs Butterworth pointed at my new lodgings. I nearly gasped.

The cottage was a charming, postcard-worthy scene. It was small and compact, but there was a warmth to it, an inviting homeliness. The thatched roof was the star of the show, its golden straws woven tightly together, standing out vividly against the lush backdrop of greenery of the woodland that stretched behind it.

A pair of wooden chairs sat invitingly outside the cottage, bathed in the soft afternoon light. They looked like the perfect place to enjoy a morning cup of tea or to watch the sunset after a day of work in the garden, and I honestly couldn't wait for those moments.

A small stone pathway led from the chairs to the front door, interspersed with tufts of wild grass and daisies. I walked towards it, the crunch of gravel under my boots mixing with the serenade of chirping birds.

I took a deep breath as I approached the front door, coloured with a subtle mint contrasting with the white-washed walls. It looked freshly painted, the colour vibrant and alive under the touch of the waning sunlight.

And then, I noticed the vines that surrounded half of the cottage. I paused and touched them, my fingers gentle on the dark leaves.

"Jasmine," I whispered and smiled. It will be blooming soon.

Jasmine Cottage. As if it was waiting here… for me.

A sign, perhaps, that I was in the right place.

My heart sped up with excitement. The garden, the cottage, summer with Jasper… after months of worrying, of million emails of rejections, and nights with no sleep, everything turned out to be better than I could have ever expected.

I turned the brass doorknob and pushed the door open. A comforting sense of warmth washed over me as I stepped inside, Mrs Butterworth right behind me. A cosy living space greeted me; its interior bathed in the glow of the setting sun pouring in from a small window. The scent of lavender and freshly baked bread filled the air, instantly making me feel at home.

I let my eyes sweep over the mint-coloured open-plan kitchen, taking in the charming aesthetic. The cupboards and work surfaces were painted a soft, refreshing, mint green, the same shade as the door, giving the room a bright and airy feel despite the small space. Gleaming copper pots and pans hung from hooks above the wooden island in the middle. A large farmhouse sink with a brass tap sat beneath a window that offered a serene view of the lush forest outside.

It was also open plan, so the plush, oatmeal-coloured sofa sat next to it. A fluffy woven rug lay in front of the fireplace, and suddenly, I imagined myself curled here with a glass of white wine and a good book.

And maybe doing some other things…

Jasmine Ackerley, focus, I scolded myself, hoping to hide a furious blush with my hair.

"It looks beautiful," I admitted to Mrs Butterworth, who busied herself with checking if I had the fresh bread and eggs.

"Ah yes, young master Jasper got this famous Cotswolds interior designer to help," Mrs Butterworth explained, triple checking and then triple checking with me if the tea supplies were sufficient. "Right," she put the eggs back into the cupboard, satisfied with her inspection. "We shall leave you to settle down. You can come to the manor house when you are done, and one of us will take you to Lord Thornvale." I nodded eagerly, my stomach fluttering with anticipation. *Lord* Thornvale.

In his ancestral home, there was no escaping Jasper's aristocratic roots.

When Parker and Mrs Butterworth left, I climbed atop the small wooden set of stairs. As I reached the top, I was met with a sight that drew yet another gasp from me; a bedroom that was breathtakingly beautiful in its simplicity. The sloping ceiling draped down to meet the wooden beams, and a huge bed was dressed in plenty of beige cushions and pillows. The entire room was bathed in a soft, mellow light filtering through the tiny window, casting an enchanting glow. A little vase was by the bed full of fragrant lilac, and I wondered who placed it there.

Caro would have laughed at me, but I was the hopeless romantic in our friendship and she was the sensible one. And although I generally tried to be more practical and hide my romantic side, it absolutely came out in full swing today. Summer days spent restoring the garden and then jasmine-scented evenings with a good book - I had no regret that I declined to go with Caro to Portugal this summer, instead taking on this job.

Then I noticed a bathtub tucked in the corner of the bedroom. An unexpected yet lovely addition to the room. My mind couldn't help but connect the dots back to Jasper. He had mentioned that he led the cottage's renovations. Had he been the one to choose this specific spot for the tub? And… was he thinking of me when he installed it, putting it by the bed?

A blush seared across my cheeks as I contemplated this possibility further. Images bloomed unbidden in my mind, innocent at first, only to veer into more bold territory. Did he picture me there naked, water droplets sliding down my skin under the warm glow of the rustic sconce lights? The thought was both terrifying and thrilling.

With a forceful shake of my head, I pulled myself from the fantasy. I wandered towards the small window.

And finally, I saw the famed Thornvale garden.

Right away, I could see that I would have a lot of work, and Jasper didn't exaggerate when he said that the garden was in disarray: it needed a loving hand. It was overgrown, utterly wild. From a neat Jacobean garden, there was nothing left; instead, a riotous sea of blooms danced in the subtle evening breeze. I opened the window wide and peered out more carefully. Closest to the house were clusters of lavender, their purple spires standing tall and proud, their potent, heady fragrance blanketing the air. Beyond them, an ocean of roses spread out, varying in shades from the deepest crimson to the softest blush pink. Near the water fountain, I spotted a collection, their elegant trumpets opening in a display of radiant whites that contrasted with algae-infused water that had a sickly green colour. But despite the obvious neglect, the garden was still breath-taking.

Especially with the sunset that had ignited the sky, the fiery reds and oranges slowly melting into soothing purples of twilight. Which reminded me I probably ought to say hello to Jasper and tell him I settled fine in the cottage.

I closed the window and glanced at the mirror: I wore blue mom jeans and a new, simple white t-shirt with a little silver necklace. For once, I let my white hair fall onto my shoulders in loose strands, curling at the ends. I looked put together, but not like I was trying too hard.

I stepped back outside and marched into the manor. I wondered if Jasper would want to hang out tonight or whether he would prefer to take things slower?

Here went my promise to prioritise job seeking and forgetting the romance.

Outside, I found Parker fixing something by the main entrance door. He greeted me and told me to follow him: apparently, Lord Thornvale was waiting for me.

The entrance hall of the Thornvale Manor was a grand spectacle, with a sweeping wooden staircase, its bannister intricately carved, winding its way up to the second floor. High above, a stunning chandelier dangled from the vaulted ceiling, its crystals winking in the light that trickled in through the mullioned windows. To one side of the hall, a massive fireplace loomed, its hearth cold and dark but nonetheless radiating a dignified charm.

As I ventured further into the house, the sound of my footsteps echoed off the rich, oak-panelled walls, the smell of old wood and time-worn stone filling the air. Dust particles floating lazily in the thin shafts of sunlight streaming through the tall, narrow windows. Despite the manor's size, there was a sense of intimacy, a feeling of being enveloped in a bygone era when the house was filled with life and laughter. That is what I remembered from childhood: this house being always full of people.

I passed rooms filled with fine antiques: heavy wooden armoires, velvet-upholstered chairs, and ornately carved tables, all evidence of the manor's rich history. Tall bookcases lined the study's walls, filled with volumes of books that bore the satisfying look of well-read tomes. Each room was a blend of faded opulence and a sense of deep-rooted history.

The beauty of the manor house was undeniable, but it was also tinged with a feeling of melancholy. Caro would have rolled her eyes at me, but I could almost hear the echo of conversations past, the rustle of silk dresses, and the clinking of crystal glasses from grand soirees. The garden rebelled and grew wilder and more untamed; inside the manor, a sense of life paused, a once vibrant household waiting to be stirred back into activity.

I was about to be a part of that, I realised, my heart pounding with excitement and trepidation. This was more than just a job. It was an opportunity to breathe life back into this grand old house to ensure its legacy continued for future generations. It was a huge responsibility, but as I stood in the heart of the Thornvale manor, I knew I was ready. This was exactly where I was meant to be

Finally, Parker stopped next to an elegant oak door.

"Lord Thornvale will see you now," he said, and with a wide smile, I entered through the door.

The first thing that I noticed was that it must have been Jasper's father's office once. There was a masculine imprint on this place: it was all very... well, dark. The walls were lined with floor-to-ceiling bookshelves, filled with volumes that ranged from worn, dog-eared tomes to immaculate, leather-bound editions. A large, mullioned window dominated one side of the office, the panes of glass slightly distorted with age, overlooking the wild, untamed garden; the big fireplace reigned at the other side.

A grand, mahogany desk stood in the heart of the office, its surface inlaid with green leather and embossed with gold. It was cluttered with an array of objects - an antique brass lamp, a crystal inkwell, and a set of faded maps strewn across one corner. An imposing, high-backed chair sat behind the desk, its dark, polished wood standing in stark contrast against the soft, worn leather seat.

And then, my whole body tensed.

Because the man in the seat was not Jasper Thornvale. His arms were folded as he stared at me with what I could only describe as mild annoyance.

"Where is... Lord Thornvale?" I asked, confused.

The man faced me with his piercing dark blue eyes, the colour of the night-time sky during storm. His features were sharp, chiselled like they were from stone, his aura exuding an intimidating elegance.

"*I* am the Lord Thornvale."

Chapter 6

This wasn't what I expected.

"W-what?" was all I mustered, utterly confused. I vaguely remembered Jasper had two uncles on his mother's side, but this man appeared only a few years older than me - not exactly my parents' age.

Suddenly, a thought formed in my head, an echo of the past trying to tell me something…

Somehow, he looked familiar, but I couldn't place him.

Meanwhile, the man continued staring at me, his intense gaze never leaving my face. A moment of surprise flickered across his stormy eyes before his expression hardened back into a cool, detached mask. He stood up and walked towards me, his hand outstretched to shake mine:

"Heath Thornvale. I take it you don't remember me," he said, a slight mockery laced with arrogance in his tone. His voice was low, like a rumble of a distant thunder.

The shock of recognition ran through me.

Oh no.

This was Jasper's older brother.

I *did* remember him. Vaguely, at least. I remembered Sienna and Jasper's brother who never wanted to hang out with his younger siblings and their friends. I remember we played some pranks on him, and I remembered a broody, angry teen who shooed us away whenever we crossed his path. I recalled some incident with hair gel being replaced with honey and how furious he was at us.

But this was no grumpy teenager. Heath radiated an air of control that left me feeling off-balance.

"I'm, um, Jasmine," I stammered. "The new gardener?"

"Ah," he said, raising an eyebrow in an entirely too attractive way. "The plant whisperer." I wanted to throw my previous thought about his attractiveness out of the window because his comment felt like a mockery.

"Well, I wouldn't exactly put it on my resume, but yes," I retorted drily.

"I do remember you. Sienna's little friend." This time, there was nothing negative in his voice, just a simple lack of interest.

"I… yes. That's me." We stared at each other in the moment that perfectly encapsulated the awkward silence. Where Jasper had this comforting, easy-going presence around him, Heath was icy cold and wore his confidence like armour. With his stiff demeanour, shirt and suit trousers, black hair neatly cut short and pale complexion, Heath Thornvale looked nothing like Jasper. The only similarity I could see were the blue eyes, but even then, Heath's eyes were a cool blue of a midnight lake, contrasting to the warmth I'd seen in Jasper's.

"Seeing that you are surprised by my presence, I take it you didn't read Jasper's email." Heath pointed out and returned to his seat.

"Err.."

Wait, what email?

Was there another email from Jasper that I didn't look at?

Emails. Stupid emails. Why is it always *emails* with me?

The thing was, I did read the email from Jasper - the one from a week ago in which he confirmed my employment and said he was looking forward to seeing me during the summer. I hadn't checked my emails since, content with all the information he sent me.

"Jasper emailed to tell you he was urgently called to Rome - some problems with his art gallery. He also left you all the directions and instructions in the email. I wanted to meet with you today to check if everything was clear but seeing as you haven't read the email..." he sank deeper into the chair, placing one leg over the other.

"I'm sorry. I will read it tonight," I blurted out, chastised. Not a great first day in the important job. I could feel my phone in my pocket, burning with that unread email.

"Good. If anything is unclear, I am happy to assist you. But generally, this is Jasper's... project: I am busy with my own work, so I'd rather you bother him with any questions," I sensed hostility there, the way he spat out the word *project*. Heath was angry at his brother, likely because Jasper employed me without Heath's approval.

Yup. Things were going from bad to worse.

"Just make sure the hydrangeas don't die," he said coolly, returning his attention to the papers on his desk. "They're my favourite."

Great. Just great. Not only did he not want me here, but he also clearly had zero faith in my gardening skills.

I could only hope that Jasper would be gone for a couple of weeks maximum - I didn't dare to ask his grumpy older brother that.

"Of course," I replied drily. "Is there anything else I should be aware of?"

"The rest is in the email." He replied pointedly.

"Sure. The email. If that's all, I'll get back to my evening."

He nodded slowly, his attention now entirely on the stack of papers. Without another word, I walked towards the door, my face burning with humiliation. I yearned to be back in my cottage.

"Oh, and Ackerley," he called out, and I bristled at him using my last name. I was his sister's childhood friend, not some random employee his brother had brought in. "The title gets passed from father to the oldest son. So *I* am the only Lord Thornvale."

Ouch.

"Goodnight," I spun around to face him. "Lord Thornvale," I added pointedly. And then I turned back around and shut the door behind me.

Parker was nowhere to be found; neither was Mrs Butterworth. I skulked around the manor house, trying to remember which way I came from. Relieved when I finally found the main door, I quickly walked outside. My heart was pounding heavily, and I welcomed the cool air of early evening.

I nearly ran back to the cottage; the world was veiled in unfamiliar darkness, and I stumbled couple of times. When I reached it, I closed the door, kicked the shoes off and ran upstairs to my suitcase. There, I had a bottle of white Chardonnay that I took with me for any emergencies, which this situation fitting the criteria for one. I took it downstairs, poured myself a hearty glass and put the rest in the fridge. Taking a gulp and ignoring the fact it was warm, I collapsed onto the sofa.

"The rest is in the email," I grumbled, mocking Heath's imperious tone. I crossed my legs and got my phone out.

I was ready to open my inbox when I suddenly heard something. I stiffened and frowned. I strained my ears, trying to locate the source of the noise. After a moment of silence, I convinced myself it was just the wind rustling the leaves outside. Unfamiliar surroundings, I said to myself.

And then the sound echoed again.

This was a big estate. I did lock the cottage using the key that Parker gave me, but what if someone crept in somehow anyway? Or worse - this was an old cottage... What if it was haunted? I imagined an old, angry ghost crawling down the stairs...

Sick with fear, I glanced around. I wanted to move and put on more lights, given that I only lit a small lamp by the sofa and the rest of the cottage was drenched in darkness.

The sound of something - *someone* - moving again. I shifted to peer into the black void in front of me.

And then, a pair of eyes staring at me from the darkness.

I shrieked and jumped out of the sofa, the remains of the white wine sloshing onto my new t-shirt.

And then... a low hiss.

Oh no - a ghost then!

Fear gripped my stomach, and I stumbled towards the kitchen. This would just be my luck: instead of a hot summer romance with the lord of the manor, I get his grumpy older brother and a haunted cottage.

I spun around, ready to grab a broom that was the closest weapon within my reach, however silly the broom against the ghost would be. And then, the movement caught my eye. Something ghost-white, yes, but small and soft and...

"Buttons?"

The cat meowed.

"Buttons!" I collapsed onto the floor, and the cat happily came to me, nuzzling my hand. "Buttons, you scared me to death!" I wasn't so ready to forgive the cat, agreeing with Parker that the bloody thing was completely out of control. But his fur was so soft that I reached out to touch him despite myself. Buttons purred happily.

Finally, I stood up and took a deep inhale.

"Stay here," I told the cat and crept upstairs to the bedroom, where I put the small light on and quickly changed into my pyjamas, tossing away the soaked t-shirt. I took my bag to the bathroom downstairs and washed off my face. Feeling a bit more like a human being, I opened the fridge and poured myself another glass of wine.

"Desperate times," I told the cat, who was staring at me somewhat judgementally from the floor. "So *this* is your secret hiding place," I scooped him from the floor and, trying to steady my shaking legs, I limped back to the sofa. The wine was still warm, and the cat looked a bit ghostly, but this situation was much better than an evil intruder or a vengeful spirit.

When I opened my inbox, there was indeed an unread email from Jasper. In it, he apologised, saying that the artist who was supposed to be shown at the gallery's opening had a breakdown and decided not to paint anymore. Jasper attached the additional thoughts and old documents from the manor's archives that could help me with re-designing the garden. In the end, he said he was so sorry again and added he was planning to return in mid-July at the latest.

"Mid-July," I closed my eyes and took another gulp of the warm Chardonnay.

That meant I was stuck here with the ghostly cat and the aloof Heath Thronvale, who clearly didn't want me here.

Oh, yes, and a long-overgrown garden which, I began to realise, would probably benefit from at least three gardeners. I had to admit that I might have bitten more than I could chew. I typed a text to Caro requesting an emergency Facetime tomorrow evening.

"I'm in trouble," I announced my increasingly precarious situation to Buttons. But the cat was now curled on my lap, fast asleep, blissfully ignorant of the humans' woes.

Chapter 7

Blindsided by a supernova sunbeam slicing through the paper-thin curtains, my eyelids flinched open. I woke up to the chirping of birds and the soft morning light that painted the delicate vines adorning the curtains, bringing out the instantly soothing charm of the little cottage. I have spent many nights scrolling through TikTok, my eyes glittering at all the cottagecore videos, presenting that perfect countryside life with a rustic cottage, slow mornings and a connection to nature. This morning felt like falling into one of those videos.

My thoughts shot back to my disastrous meeting with Heath Thornvale. Heath, with his inscrutable midnight blue eyes. Heath with his "I don't give two hoots about you" attitude that still stung like a lash of nettles. Heath, looking like he'd just walked out of a broody historical drama. Really, the only thing missing was the thunderous sky behind him.

Okay, I had to stop romanticising him. After our meeting last night, the only description that he deserved was: Heath Thornvale, a complete arse.

Rubbing my temples, I swung my legs off the bed. Stretching, I caught sight of the brass-framed mirror. My own bleary-eyed, wild-haired reflection glared back, a stark reminder of yesterday's whirlwind introduction to

Thornvale Manor. Truth be told, I resembled a raccoon who'd survived a tornado.

And then, a flash of white darted across the bedroom. I jumped, scrambling backwards into the dubious safety of the bedroom. A soft, mocking "meow" echoed from the stairs. Buttons, of course, seemed to have a penchant for scaring any Thornvale Manor guests.

"Buttons!" I folded my arms. "You are clearly not a ghost, or at least I hope you're not. Can you stop just…appearing from nowhere?" The cat paused, its sapphire eyes gleaming as it fixed a judgmental stare at me. Then, it let out a satisfied purr, turned tail, and sauntered off, its point made.

I groaned again, burying my face in my hands. I was in the heart of a romantic horror novel. Only the hero was a snob, the ghost was a cat, and the heroine… well, she really needed a cup of tea and a hot shower. And perhaps a manual on how to survive at Thornvale Manor.

Surprisingly, despite the odd meeting with Heath last night and Buttons attempting to scare me to death, I slept well. The bed was comfortable, and so was the silence, no noise of cars that frequented my parent's house or the general cityscape sounds that I was so used to in my London flat. I also hoped that Parker would find Buttons and finally get peace of mind over the unruly cat, which would be at least one positive development in this last twenty four hours.

I texted Caro about the time for Facetime later in the evening and told my parents all was well, which, of course, it wasn't, but I had no intention of worrying them. They were both so excited about me working in the Thornvale Manor I had no heart to dampen their excitement, even if mine was withering like a rose without the water.

Still, I made myself look less like a tornado-touched racoon and walked outside into the fresh, sunny morning. I stared at the vast expanse of the garden from the threshold of my cottage, a mixed palette of greenery and splashes of colour. The rush of anticipation pulsed in my veins.

I was finally back at gardening.

I hauled on my gardening boots and gloves. Striding through the undergrowth, my boots crunched on fallen leaves and unidentified garden debris. It featured a long dead mouse, which I imagined was Buttons' dinner.

The remnants of the garden's impressive grandeur were there, of course, but it was hard to focus on them given its general state. The beautifully crafted arches were now draped in untamed vines, the labyrinthine hedges that now looked more like something from a nightmare, the symmetrical beds that were once a pride of Jacobean garden were now a buffet for every weed known to mankind. A decorative pond had been transformed into a green soup with more algae than water. And there, in the middle of the chaos, sat a lonely statue of a cherub, its chubby face caked with grime, and the once-shimmering fountain now spitting out water with the enthusiasm of a three-day-old soda. The lone statue of a Greek god in the corner was now sporting a fine moustache of ivy.

I pinched the bridge of my nose and exhaled. Jasper said it would be a challenge. He said it needed a bit of work, that it was neglected. Only neglected felt like a vast understatement. He failed to mention that it needed a reality TV show intervention, a miracle, and possibly an exorcism.

"Well, well, well," I sighed, hands planted on my hips, my eyes scanning the snarl of unkempt foliage, "if it isn't the Secret Garden's less fortunate cousin."

Worry gnawed at me - the garden was vast and in a bad shape. Still, a smile tugged at the corners of my mouth. There was a thrill in the prospect of taming the wild, of restoring a piece of history to its former glory, even if it was an overgrown Jacobean mess. I reached out and touched a wayward, newly blooming climbing rose, its apricot-yellow petals velvety against my gloves.

Bathsheba, this particular species was called.

A beautiful choice.

Wasting no time, I got to work. The first order of business was to get the lay of the land, so I set off with a notepad and my small camera, ready to document every nook and cranny of the gardens. I wanted to understand the essence of the place, see how the light fell, listen to the rhythm of the wind rustling through the trees, and observe the movement of the wildlife. As a gardener and a landscape designer, I was taught to approach a project like this with a healthy amount of respect for the existing ecosystem.

I walked the pathways first, old stone worn smooth by the passage of time, with tufts of weed. They snaked through the vast lawns, lined with various trees, shrubs, and flowers in various states of growth and neglect. I jotted down notes, clicked photos, and imagined how to breathe life back into space. Or rather, how could I tame the liveliness of the garden?

Next, I explored the more secluded areas of the garden – the rose arbour that had seen better days, the dilapidated greenhouse begging for a touch of love, and a hidden garden statue half-consumed by an overly ambitious ivy. It was like piecing together a puzzle, seeing how each part connected to the whole.

By midday, I was halfway through my exploration, munching on a sandwich while seated on an old stone bench under the shade of a grand willow tree. I skipped breakfast, and Mrs Butterworth, surely possessing some magical abilities, materialised just before noon with a tray full of sandwiches, crisps and homemade biscuits.

"I could hear your stomach rumbling from the kitchen," she shook her head disapprovingly. "Jasmine, I did say if you wanted any breakfast-"

"I'll come to have breakfast in the manor tomorrow, I promise. And after that, I planned to pop into

Sagebourne - I need a couple of things from the garden centre. I can get some of the breakfast things for myself then." I said, hushing Mrs Butterworth's protests that I could join them for breakfast every day. It felt almost too generous, and besides, I liked cooking for myself and was looking forward to using cottage's charming utensils.

Sipping some lemonade and watching Mrs Butterworth trailing back to the kitchen, my eyes fell back into the garden.

A strange feeling surrounded the overgrown greenery: sadness of being neglected, yes, but also anger. It sounded strange, even for a hopeless romantic like me, but I had this palpable feeling of the garden being furious about being left to fend for itself. Anger of something once so loved that was cruelly discarded.

I remembered running around the gardens with Jasper, Sienna and some of the other village children. I recalled the photos Jasper sent me, of village fetes and garden parties frequently held in the Thornvale Manor, of the garden blooming, healthy and looked after, full of life and laughter. It was still full of life, but the laughter has long died.

I supposed it must have died with Edward Thornnvale.

A sudden surge of sorrow tightened my throat, even though I didn't know him well.

I vaguely remembered him as a gregarious, funny man who always had lots of hilarious stories to tell and once helped us steal some cake from the kitchen when Mrs Butterworth wasn't looking. The rest I heard from Mum: how everyone loved the Thornvales, how the Thornvale Manor used to be the centre of the town. How Margot Thornvale was more into art and put her effort into Sagebourne's community centre and little art gallery, and how Eddie Thornvale loved throwing parties and connecting with people. How no one would ever think, save for his accent, that he was the lord of the manor when they met him. I didn't know much about what happened after Eddie Thornvale passed away - I was in my final year in London's sixth form, but after aggressive cancer claimed him, there was no party thrown at Thornvale Manor ever again.

Before I let myself get overwhelmed with sadness and anxiety, I cleared up after myself, determined even more to fulfil Jasper's wish and restore the garden to its former glory.

The afternoon was dedicated to the more serious part of the job - taking soil samples and noting the areas that needed immediate attention. Finally, I grabbed a blanket, put it over the wooden chairs outside the Jasmine Cottage, and settled down there with some peppermint tea, my laptop, and the garden design plans.

I already spent some time going over the historical research, immersing myself in books, articles, and archival materials to learn about the design principles, plant selections, and features commonly found in Jacobean gardens. With Jasper's help, I also obtained historical maps, engravings, and photographs to gather visual references and inspiration to finally create a loose garden design concept that Jasper already approved of. Now, after spending the day looking over the garden, I started working on the renders and sketches, hoping to send them to Jasper as soon as possible so I can move on to the next phase: clearing and pruning. I opened my calendar, added a couple more days to finalise my design plan, and then closed it with a thud. The last twenty-four hours were a whirlwind, and tiredness was fast catching up with me.

Just as the evening settled over the Thornvale Manor, I grabbed my plans and headed back to the cottage. Getting myself more tea and preparing a quick sandwich, I connected to Caro on Facetime. She picked up after one ringtone, and her tanned skin, dark straight hair and a wide grin came into view on my phone screen.

"Ahh, my favourite gardener!" she greeted me, and I waved at her before taking my phone and getting comfy on the sofa.

"How's Portugal? And more importantly, how's Roberto?" I grinned at my friend. Caro started to laugh and told me about her new flat in Portugal, where she moved to this last week, and Roberto, her new Portuguese crush and a waiter in her local beach club. I admired Caro's new tattoo of her favourite corgi, and we tried to decipher whether Roberto's charming smiles meant that he was interested in Caro or simply being polite.

"Right, enough about me," Caro took a sip of Aperol and gave me a critical look. "I want to know how your romance with the sexy lord of the manor is going, because I hope you at least shared a passionate kiss amongst the roses or something like that."

I sighed dramatically, a sense of sadness washing over me. Before I accepted Jasper's offer of employment, I planned to go with Caro to spend the summer in Lisbon, flirting with locals and having ungodly amounts of Aperol. I was quickly regretting not holding on to that promise.

"Elaborate on that sigh, please," Caro commanded.

"I just wish I went with you," I confessed. "Because everything here went sideways. The garden, I am telling you, easily requires three full-time gardeners - I don't know what I was thinking about when I accepted the job. There is a ghostly cat who nearly scared me to death last night, and oh, instead of Prince Charming, I ended up with his older brother, Count Dracula," I concluded miserably.

"There is a lot to unpack in this sentence," she glanced at her drink, "and not enough Aperol." She turned back with another glass. "Firstly, what's wrong with Count Dracula? I know you were always more of an Edward Cullen fan, but still…"

I explained to Caro how I missed Jasper's final email and my disastrous meeting with his older brother.

"Well, that sounds positively delightful," Caro remarked, her face suddenly pixelated on my screen thanks to the bad connection, a smirk plainly heard in her voice. "Just like in one of those romantic comedies, you know, where the guy and the girl hate each other at first?"

I gave her a look. "Yes, except this is real life, and Heath is less 'charmingly misunderstood' and more 'aggravatingly apathetic.' He doesn't seem to care about the garden at all."

"So let me get this straight," she began, her eyes dancing with amusement. "You, the 'Urban Landscaping Goddess,' met the 'Country Bumpkin' Heath, and things didn't go exactly as planned?"

I glared at the screen, trying to maintain some semblance of dignity. "Well, when you put it that way, it sounds ridiculous."

She shrugged, a smirk playing on her lips. "Did it not happen that way?"

"I wouldn't exactly say 'Country Bumpkin'," I sighed. "More like 'Horticulturally-Challenged Heath'. I grimaced at the memory of our disastrous meeting. "And he doesn't care about the garden. It's like the garden doesn't exist, except, of course, it does, and it's so overgrown it practically started to enter the house. I literally think the weeds have established their own government at this point."

Caro burst into laughter, nearly spilling her freshly refilled. "I can picture it now. The Battle of the Backyard: Jasmine versus The Weed Republic."

I glared at Caro in mock annoyance, but a grim thought had already taken root inside me.

This was going to be a loooong summer.

Chapter 8

I arrived in Thornvale Manor ready for breakfast, keeping my promise to Mrs Butterworth. I dressed up for the occasion in my blue dress, with a nice sweetheart neckline and buttoned-up back, which proved to be a pain, but in the end made me feel less like a gardener and more like… well, like a gardener who was attending breakfast in the fancy country manor.

I said my hellos to Parker and Mrs Butterworth, who gestured at me to go to the place they called a morning room, where breakfast was normally served.

As I entered the morning room, the warm aroma of freshly brewed coffee mingled with the sweet scent of pastries. The sun cast a gentle glow through the large windows, casting dappled patterns on the polished wooden floor.

And there he was, seated at the far end of the table. Count Dracula… sorry, Heath Thornvale. The soft morning light accentuated his strong, chiselled features and he was already dressed in a dark, tailored suit.

"Good morning," I cleared my throat, shuffling towards the other side of the table.

"Morning," he responded, his eyes briefly flickering to me before returning to his laptop placed next to his coffee, page opened on the list of unanswered emails.

I don't know why I was so shocked to see him there. Didn't Mrs Butterworth mention having breakfast in the manor with Lord Thornvale? I was pretty sure she did. Only then I was excited to share my breakfast with the *other* brother.

I grabbed some toast and jam, pouring fresh tea and orange juice, trying to steady my shaking hands.

I sat at the breakfast table with Heath, feeling the weight of the awkward silence pressing against my chest. We had barely exchanged a few words since we sat down, and I couldn't help but fidget with my napkin, desperately trying to think of something to say. Our last encounter wasn't exactly ideal, and I wondered if I should give him another chance. After all, I needed him on my side, seeing as he was the only manor's owner on site, with Jasper away in Rome. Who knows, maybe I would get through that stone-cold exterior, and we would at least be able to collaborate with each other.

I nervously cleared my throat, searching for something to say. "So, uh...the breakfast is lovely. Mrs Butterworth is a very talented cook."

"She is." A reply, followed by the silence again and the sound of clicking as he responded to the email.

"Have you tried the jam? It's, uh, really good," I stammered, pointing awkwardly at the jar in the middle of the table. Why did I have to be stuck with the brother who was not easy to talk to?

Heath glanced at me, a pained expression crossing his face. "Yes, it's very good," he replied curtly, quickly diverting his eyes back to the newspaper on the table.

Right, I ran out of the cooking compliments as a viable conversation starter.

"I, um, heard the weather forecast is calling for rain later today," I blurted out, mentally cringing at my own banality.

Heath sighed audibly; his frustration evident. He folded the newspaper and looked me straight in the eyes. "Look, Ackerley, I appreciate the effort, but I really prefer to enjoy my breakfast in silence," he said with finality, his tone slightly exasperated.

"Oh, yes. Of course," I responded, watching him get back to his emails, marginally hurt.

At least I tried to be friendly again. He was, after all, my childhood friends' brother. And I tried to make an effort.

But this was the last time. Heath Thornvale clearly wanted nothing but to keep this relationship as distant and professional as possible.

Fine with me.

I gobbled down my breakfast and left the table with a polite but cold "have a good day" to Heath, to which he responded with the same, not even looking at me.

Despite the breakfast fiasco, I woke up in a good mood, cheered by my conversation with Caro last night. I was determined to stay in a good mood and let myself be excited about my renders that I hoped I could send to Jasper for final approval later today. No wallowing in negativity.

After grabbing my laptop and notebooks from the cottage, I returned to the manor. The skies looked dark grey, and in his email, Jasper told me to use the drawing room for my work, should I want to. And I thought that given the weather and more of a desk-based part of the job, the opportunity to work in a manor had indeed presented itself today.

I settled into the plush armchair in the manor's elegant drawing room, surrounded by shelves of dusty books and timeless works of art. My sketchbook lay on the mahogany coffee table, filled with intricate designs and colourful illustrations of the garden I envisioned for Thornvale Manor.

As I worked on my sketches, my favourite ABBA tunes filled the room, the lively melodies creating an atmosphere of playful energy. Soon enough, I was singing happily.

Maybe more than just singing happily.

"Dancing Queeeeeen!" I belted out. At the same time, the door opened, cutting my singing short.

My heart skipped a beat as Heath stood there, framed in the doorway, his eyes scanning the room with a cool intensity that sent shivers down my spine.

"Ackerley," he frowned, sweeping his eyes across the room, "what exactly are you doing?"

"Finalising my sketches," I replied. "And listening to ABBA," I added, turning the music down. "You are welcome to look at the sketches if you want."

"I would like you to take your work back to your cottage, please."

I frowned. I was *sure* that in my email, Jasper was more than happy for me to use the rooms in the manor for my work. "But Jasper said-"

"Jasper is not here, is he? And I have... an important guest coming up in thirty minutes," he scowled as if he wasn't particularly thrilled by said guest. "So I'd like to ask you to leave."

As I gathered my belongings and rose from the armchair, I couldn't help but feel a tinge of sadness. The vibrant atmosphere I had created in the room, filled with the lively tunes of ABBA, seemed to dissipate with Heath's presence.

"You know what, Thornvale, you really are the master of sucking the life out of a room," I said before I was able to stop the words leaving my lips.

Ooops. So much for keeping things professional.

But Heath only arched an eyebrow. "And here I thought it was the music that was doing the trick," he retorted.

"ABBA? Never! Well, consider yourself lucky. You're getting a taste of the lively side of life for once. I bet it's a refreshing change from your usual brooding vampire routine," I quipped, moving past him. As I did so, he leaned towards me, his lips brushing against my ears.

"Ah, so you've discovered my secret," I shivered. And then he moved back again, stepping into the room. He glanced outside the window, presumably checking if his guest had turned up, before he faced me again and said coldly: "I suppose my vampire tendencies do come in handy when I need a quiet room for important meetings."

"They really are remarkably good," I mumbled.

"Consider this room occupied for the rest of your employment contract."

I pinched my lips together and glared at him but refused to drag this conversation further. I withdrew from the drawing room, heading towards the main entrance where I left my rainproof jacket. Outside the manor I was greeted by the cold, grey day that appeared to depart completely from sunny days of early June that we have been having so far.

It was drizzling, as well, but I didn't mind it. The rain was cooling the feelings that I had towards Heath. No, not feelings. One, very particular feeling.

Anger. I was angry at Heath Thornvale for being uncaring, cold and dismissive, angry in the same lively, untamed way the garden was.

When I sat down at the cottage's kitchen aisle with my laptop and my sketches, I forced myself to focus, working on my plans for the rest of the day. Sometime during the day, the white Bentley that turned up after I was banished from the manor left - I guessed it must have been Heath's client. I understood very little about his job, but it appeared to be finance related. With the arrival of twilight, I sent Jasper an email detailing my concepts and asking for a final approval before the work would start.

To my surprise, Jasper's email pinged only an hour later. He loved the plans and was keen for me to start turning my plans into reality from as early as tomorrow. I smiled at the email and his enthusiasm; my smile widened when I reached the ending, where he once again apologised for not being there and expressed his excitement for seeing me in July.

I looked over the day's work with a sense of accomplishment. I had a plan now, a vision of what the garden could become. It would take time, patience, and a lot of hard work, but I was up for the challenge.

And there was no way I would let Heath Thornvale ruin it.

Chapter 9

The next day, I prioritised getting to Sagebourne, stopping by some grocery shopping before going to the local garden centre. I couldn't drive, but despite noticing a garage full of luxury cars, I refused to ask Heath for help. I just had to be careful not to miss my bus. Besides, most things that I asked Jasper to get were already delivered and waiting in the greenhouse, so I only needed a new pair of gardening gloves and some new pruners.

By the time I arrived in town, he cobblestone streets were bustling with activity, small shops lining the way, their facades bearing the wear of time but undeniably maintaining a sort of rustic appeal. Brightly painted wooden signs swayed gently in the breeze, advertising fresh produce, artisanal crafts, and homemade pastries. The scent of freshly baked bread wafted through the air, mingling with the faint aroma of blooming flowers from the nearby park. It was a lovely place, and I could see why my parents never wanted to move.

I reached Eden Garden Centre, ready to pick up everything I needed.

"Jasmine, is that you?" A warm, familiar voice called out. I turned to see Rosemary, the garden centre manager, bustling towards me, her face lighting up with a genuine smile.

Rosemary was a gardening guru in these parts. Her knowledge about plants and flowers was almost legendary. Her curly grey hair was tied back into a loose bun, wisps escaping around her face. Despite her age, her energy was infectious, her love for plants evident in every gesture and word. She was away for the past few months, caring for her elderly mother, whom she eventually brought back to the care home nearby Sagebourne.

"What's new, Jasmine? How is job searching going?"

"Not bad, actually. Got a job at Thornvale Manor." I replied, pride swelling inside me.

Rosemary's eyes widened. "Thornvale Manor? Now, that's a place that could use a good gardener. The poor gardens there have been neglected for far too long."

"I agree. That's why I'm there, to bring them back to life, "I said, my determination seeping into my words.

Rosemary hummed thoughtfully, looking at me with a new sense of respect. "Well, it won't be an easy task. But if anyone can do it, it's you, my dear. You always had a knack for making things grow. What a shame, though. I remember all of the garden parties there… it was simply magical," her eyes glazed briefly with memories before she blinked and smiled at me. "Anyway, I ought to stop wasting your time. Let me get you what you need. And do keep me updated about your progress - who knows, maybe Thornvale children will open their doors for the local community again."

I smiled and nodded, doubt heavy in my chest. With Sienna doing a career in London and with Jasper's investments requiring him to travel a lot, that left Heath. And he made it very clear he had no interest in the garden, let alone about reaching out to the local community. I doubted Rosemary's wish would ever be granted.

This time, I kept my eye on time and returned to Thornvale Manor after successfully catching the bus.

As it was barely past lunchtime, I wasted no time to get started. Gloves on, tools at the ready, I stood on the edge of the overgrown wilderness of the Thornvale Manor garden, sizing up my verdant opponent. As I flexed my fingers in my gloves, the smell of earth and foliage filled my nostrils, an intoxicating aroma that gave me an adrenaline jolt.

The battle commenced. I began hacking away at the undergrowth, each snip of the shears a triumphant shout in the silent, green wilderness. Sweat trickled down my face, my muscles ached, and my back screamed obscenities. But I soldiered on.

Just as I was congratulating myself on my progress, something caught my eye. There, on the edge of the garden, was a squirrel. And in its tiny paws was something that looked suspiciously familiar. My heart sank as I recognized my only spare pair of gardening gloves.

"No way," I muttered, squinting at the scene. The squirrel cocked its head, holding the gloves as if it had just won a prize at the world's smallest carnival. Then, it bolted towards the trees, my gloves bouncing comically in its mouth.

"Hey!" I shouted, dropping my shears and chasing after it. The squirrel darted left and right, my gloves swinging from its mouth like a ridiculous cartoon flag. "Those are mine, you tiny bandit!"

I skidded around a tree just in time to see the squirrel dodging into a hole, my gloves disappearing with it. I stared at the empty hole, panting, incredulous.

"That's just perfect," I grumbled, hands on my hips. "Of everything to steal, it had to be my gloves. What's it going to do with them anyway? Start a squirrel gardening club?"

Despite the unexpected glove theft, the sight of my partially cleared garden made me smile. Sure, I had lost a pair of gloves to a kleptomaniac squirrel, but I could also see a little patch of the garden that looked… lovely. Or well looked after, at least.

I spent the next few days continuing with the pruning and weeding, progress being slow but continuous. I preferred to cook for myself, but Mrs Butterworth promised a fantastical full English on

Saturday, and even the presence of Heath couldn't keep me away from that.

Indeed, Heath was already there, and I noticed two things: one, that his plate looked as if he was about to finish his breakfast, which was good news because it didn't mean we had to talk to each other very much if he was about to leave. And he certainly looked like he had some work to do, given that he was wearing a suit on Saturday. His cold, piercing eyes were glued to some sort of work document rather than acknowledging the presence of a guest - namely, me. The man was as warm as an iceberg and twice as inviting.

We continued our silent breakfast, me battling my eggs benedict, him wrestling with his precious papers. As soon as I was full, I returned to my cottage. Putting on my old grey t-shirt and denim shorts, I got ready to work.

Today, I hoped to prune and clean the dahlias, which have mercifully stayed within their flower beds. I hoped it would be a nice task for Saturday, easier than battling through the weeds in the rest of the garden.

The sight of the dahlias should cheer me up, but not this time. I stepped closer and my heart sank. The usually robust, healthy leaves bore ugly, brownish spots as though they were stricken by some sort of plant acne. This was not good.

"Bacterial leaf spots. Great," I grumbled, examining the spotted leaves with the precision of a seasoned detective. I've read about them in gardening books, but this was my first encounter with this dreaded enemy in the real garden. "Nothing like a good old-fashioned bacterial invasion to ruin your day."

I plucked a leaf and held it up against the sunlight. The spots stood out like graffiti on a clean wall. I googled bacterial leaf spot to double-check, but I was sadly right. And that meant I needed to order the antibacterial treatment for them, or there would be little left of the poor dahlias.

Resigned, I realised it meant discussing the matter with Heath. I couldn't risk waiting for Jasper to respond – I needed that treatment now.

I found Heath in his office (no surprise there), engrossed in a ledger (also no surprise there). He was seated in his enormous leather chair, his brows knitted together as he scanned the pages.

"Do you have a moment?" I asked, stopping in front of him.

Without looking up, he replied curtly, "Not really."

Despite his response, I pressed on. The survival of the dahlias depended on it. "The dahlias are showing signs of bacterial leaf spot. We need to take immediate action, or we might lose them."

Finally, he glanced up from his ledger. "Can't you handle it, Jasmine? Isn't that what we hired you for?"

His dismissive tone sent a wave of frustration through me. "Yes, but I need to order some specific antibacterial treatments, and they're not cheap. I need your approval."

He waved his hand in a nonchalant gesture, eyes already returning to the ledger. "Do whatever you think is best. Just don't go over budget that you have discussed with my brother."

Annoyance bubbled up in me. It wasn't about the budget. It was about him taking an interest, showing some semblance of care about the manor's grounds. "This is your family's legacy. Doesn't it matter to you?"

Heath sighed, closing the ledger with a snap. His eyes locked onto mine. "Right now, what matters to me is making sure we have the funds to maintain this 'legacy'. If you can't understand that, then it's not my problem."

He stood up abruptly, leaving me alone in his office. His disinterest was more than just irritating; it was disappointing.

I shouldn't care about the garden or Heath's attitude: I was only there as an employee.

But strangely, I did.

Chapter 10

My first Sunday in Thornvale Manor brought something pleasantly unexpected: an email with a job alert.

As the relentless rain drummed a steady rhythm against the windowpane, I found myself huddled in the Jasmine Cottage. I hoped to do some work on the garden, but the rain was incessant, and I gave up after getting drenched and cold in the first hour.

Which was how I ended up with Mrs Butterworth's ginger tea, staring at my laptop screen and the job posting. The position was with one of the city's leading landscaping companies, known for creating lush, vibrant green spaces amid the concrete and steel of the capital. It was an exciting prospect, and my heart did a small flip at the thought of going back.

The rolling green hills and the scent of roses might be replaced by manicured city parks and the occasional waft of roasted chestnuts from a street vendor, but that was a trade-off I was beginning to consider. And let's not forget the prospect of working on a variety of projects, each with their own unique challenges and rewards.

As I began to fill out the online application, I couldn't help but feel a sense of exhilaration. It made my fingers fly across the keyboard, pouring my heart and soul into every response.

Gardening in the city would be a far cry from Thornvale Manor's sprawling, unruly garden, with its stubborn knot gardens and temperamental water features. And perhaps more appealing was the idea of leaving behind the equally stubborn, if not more so, Heath Thornvale. His chilly demeanour and sharp tongue were as much a part of the Thornvale landscape as the age-old oaks and the ornamental yew hedges, and most definitely less welcomed.

I could exchange the icy mornings at the breakfast table with Heath for the warm familiarity of an old friend's company over a weekend brunch at our favourite London café. And given my current experience in Thornvale Manor, I was sure they would look at my experience favourably.

As I hit 'Submit', a rush of adrenaline coursed through me, tinged with a hint of excitement and the thrill of potential change. I closed my laptop with a satisfying snap and stood up, stretching my stiffened muscles. Peering from the rain-speckled window, I raised my tea mug to the relentless downpour and the obstinate Jacobean garden.

Still, I couldn't ignore a pang of guilt. Sure, the London job would start towards the end of August, not really infringing on my contract with Jasper. Sure, I could still have my sizzling summer full of hot sex with Jasper, who was due to come back in four weeks. Yet, I couldn't help but think about Jasper wondering whether it was possible to extend my employment further and how I told him I would be up for it. I felt guilty my job application would be seen as deceptive.

But later in the afternoon, Heath Thornvale and his very existence managed to squash that guilt very quickly. I was standing near a patch of lilies when Heath appeared from behind the manor. Somewhat casual shirt and chinos replaced his usual pristine suit. It was, in fact, the closest to 'casual' I had ever seen him. It was a refreshing sight, but I knew better than to let my guard down.

"Morning, Thornvale," I greeted him, attempting to sound as cordial as possible, hoping I was blushing furiously.

"Ackerley," he responded, not even slowing his pace.

I took a deep breath, preparing myself. "I wanted to ask your opinion about this section," I said, gesturing towards the lilies.

He barely glanced in their direction. "I'm sure whatever you decide will be fine."

The dismissive tone in his voice felt like a slap. "You don't even know what my question is," I pointed out, irritation creeping into my tone.

He finally stopped and turned to face me, the look on his face clearly communicating his annoyance. "Does it matter? You're the gardener. You make the decisions."

It was true. I was the gardener. But this was his home, his family's legacy. Didn't he care at all? His indifference felt like an insult.

"Heath, this is your home. Your opinion matters," I insisted, trying to keep my voice steady.

"You were hired for a reason, Ackerley," he retorted. "And, may I remind you, I did not hire you. Jasper clearly trusts your judgement, and if you want an opinion, bother him. Now, if you'll excuse me, I have work to do."

With that, he turned and walked away, leaving me with frustration simmering in my veins. He might be content to abandon his responsibilities and let others make decisions for him, but I wouldn't let his indifference impact my work. The garden, the manor, deserved better. Even if the manor's own heir didn't seem to care.

Still, it squashed any remaining guilt I had for applying for the London job.

I was also still waiting for Jasper's response: I hoped he would get the antibacterial treatment for the dahlias, bypassing Heath's indifference. But so far, it seemed like Jasper's business must have been in crisis, given that days went by, and I had not heard anything.

The days continue to flow, and I started with the knot gardens. They looked like a game of pick-up sticks played by giants. The hedges gnashed their leafy teeth at my shears, but by the day's end, the first glimmers of their old shapes emerged. I started my war on the parterres, too.

Once crisp as a starched shirt, the borders had disappeared under a siege of weeds that grew faster than bamboo on steroids. With gloved hands, I pulled, yanked, wrestled, and tugged until I was sure my fingers would be permanently curled into claws. But victory was sweet, as by sunset towards the end of the week, the borders began to reappear, and the ghost of the old garden started to emerge.

Which was actually nice to see. I snapped a photo and emailed it to Jasper. I then got back to the cottage to dress for dinner with my parents. Initially, I thought about jeans and a t-shirt, but I took a lot of nice dresses and heels (I thought about spending summer with Jasper, remember), and it was a shame they were wasting away in the wardrobe. So I chose a lilac bodycon dress and nude heels, because who knows, maybe after the dinner I could explore a bit of Sagebourne nightlife. I added some mascara and lip gloss, and grabbing my bag, I gave myself an appreciative look in the mirror.

Emerging from the cottage, I slipped into the cocoon of twilight. The evening air held the gentle chill of impending night, brushing my bare arms with a goosebump-causing coolness. The manor house towered above me, its white wisteria shimmering spectrally in the dimming light.

My heels clicked rhythmically against the gravel path, the only sound breaking the silence of the evening. The only problem in my nearly fool proof plan was that I planned to walk for forty minutes to the town, given that no buses were running that late. And it was proving difficult to walk in high heels. I vowed to myself that I would use the money from this job to get a driving licence.

Just as I began my stroll towards the gate, the growl of an engine sliced through the calm. A car materialised out of the dwindling light - Heath's sleek vehicle, looking as elegant and polished as the man himself.

Rolling to a stop beside me, the window slipped down, revealing the driver. His midnight blue eyes flitted over me, sharp as a freshly forged blade. A shiver raced down my spine, a dash of excitement I absolutely refused to acknowledge.

"I'm off to dinner with my parents before you make some annoying comment," I faced him, trying to keep my voice steady despite the unexpected flutter in my stomach.

There was a heavy pause with a tension neither of us would acknowledge.

"I could give you a ride," he offered finally, popping the passenger door open with a lean of his broad shoulders. "And there was no comment I was planning to make."

"Sure," I rolled my eyes. "I'm perfectly capable of walking," I pointed out. My left heel started to sink into the gravel, and I wobbled dangerously. I yanked my foot furiously and had to use the car to stabilise myself.

Heath sighed. "I'm sure you are, but I'd rather not be the reason for your twisted ankle."

"Such Prince Charming." I scoffed, trying to regain my balance in the most graceful way.

"Why don't you let me give you a ride then, Cinderella? I am heading that way anyway."

I shot him a pointed look. "And risk turning into a pumpkin at midnight?"

The corner of his full lips twitched. "I can bring you back home before the clock strikes twelve if you want."

Despite myself, I hesitated, my gaze dropping to the open car door. I mean, it would be so much easier…

Ah, damn my pride. My heels were too expensive to waste on the road, and I risked the gravel swallowing my whole body before I even got there.

My tone dripped with sarcasm as I finally slid into the leather seat beside him. "But if you turn into a frog, I'm not kissing you."

Heath put the car in gear. "You say that now," he murmured, and my heart skipped a beat at the teasing promise in his voice.

The predatory purr of the car engine filled the air as I was sitting rigidly in the passenger seat. It was a sound that echoed the tension coiling between us.

But it seemed the tension had shifted somewhat from the previous couple of weeks. We haven't spoken at all during the car ride, apart from me thanking Heath for the ride and telling him my parents would drop me off. As I walked into the restaurant, I couldn't help but think that there was animosity between us, but it was no longer *just* animosity…

Dinner with my parents went as expected: I told myself not to babble about annoying Heath and the garden, and after one glass of wine, of course, I blabbed everything.

"Sounds like you've got yourself a real garden-variety drama there, Jasmine," Dad quipped, a playful grin on his face. We were sitting in the local Pizza Express, and I was stabbing my dough balls with considerable force after confessing to my parents that things were not going as perfectly as I expected. Still, I wasn't going to give up that easily.

I groaned, burying my face in my hands. "Dad, please."

He simply chuckled, unapologetic. "What? It's growing on you, isn't it?"

I rolled my eyes, a smile tugging at the corners of my mouth. "Very funny, Dad. But yes, something like that. It's me against Heath and the weeds, and the bacterial leaf spots, and—"

"And the squirrel that stole your gloves," Mum added, the hint of a chuckle in her voice.

"Let's not forget the squirrel," I conceded, laughing along. "Honestly, I should've stayed in the city. The only things that attacked me were deadlines and the occasional pigeon."

"Darling, this all sounds pretty dramatic," Mum winked at me.

"Fine, laugh it up," I huffed, trying to suppress my own laughter. "Just remember, when I finally conquer the garden, and it's the most beautiful sight you've ever seen, you'll eat your words."

Dad looked at me solemnly. "That's if the garden doesn't eat you first."

Chapter 11

I had no plans for this to happen. And I had no intention of giving up.

Which is why I was ready to battle the garden again.

On a Sunday morning, no less. The only day when most of the world agreed to sleep in. And what was I doing? My shiny new hedge trimmer lay before me, a beast of machinery that roared like a motorbike and cut through foliage like butter. Today's mission: to reduce the Amazonian jungle that called itself the hedge into a nice, neighbour-friendly shrubbery.

There was no way I was letting the garden win.

I yanked the cord with a triumphant tug, and the hedge trimmer roared to life. The garden birds scattered, probably filing a noise complaint with the local squirrel judiciary. The machine's growl echoed in the otherwise quiet Sunday morning.

Five minutes into my job, an agitated voice cut through the noise. I looked up, the trimmer still roaring in my hands, to see Heath hanging out his window. He looked like he'd been woken up from a century-long slumber, hair sticking out in all directions and a scowl so deep it could host its own ecosystem.

"Ackerley!" He shouted, his voice filled with an outrage. "Are you seriously doing this *now*? It's the crack of dawn on a Sunday!"

I clicked off the hedge trimmer, the silence following its roar seeming almost unnatural.

"Morning, Thornvale!" I called back cheerfully. "And it's actually nine-thirty. You might want to get your crack of dawn recalibrated."

His scowl deepened, if that were even possible. "Some people try to enjoy a bit of peace on their weekends, you know."

"Peace?" I mimed, looking around. "In this wilderness? I think the peace left when the first weeds sprouted."

He just stared at me, the disbelief on his face clear even from the distance. "Could you at least... I don't know, use a less demonic device?"

"I could," I agreed amiably, patting the hedge trimmer. "But where's the fun in that?" I flashed my teeth at him. The poor dahlias had no peace from their bacterial infection; there was no way Heath Thornvale would be granted that privilege.

He disappeared back into his house. I chuckled, cranking the machine back to life, its deafening roar echoing through the sleepy Sunday morning.

Served him right. No opinions and no help with the garden? Fine. But I would take no complaints either.

***

It was a bright Thursday morning, and I was up to my elbows in roses. Armed with a pair of heavy-duty gardening gloves and the kind of determination only a person fighting with a garden could understand, I set about taming the wild climbers that had taken the south wall hostage.

Each thorny tendril seemed to have a mind of its own and a stubborn one at that, much like the owner of Thornvale Manor. The image of Heath's usual stern, unyielding expression floated into my mind, making me shake my head as I tried to focus on the task.

Suddenly, movement in the corner of my eye made me glance up. The window to Heath's room was usually shut tight, the thick curtains drawn against the world outside. But today, it was wide open and standing there, framed in the glow of the morning sunlight, was Heath himself.

To say I was taken aback would be an understatement. He was fresh from the shower, with nothing but a towel hanging low around his hips. Droplets of water glistened on his chest, trickling down the well-defined muscles of his abdomen to disappear beneath the edge of the towel.

Our eyes locked, and the world seemed to still. I was frozen in place, shears in hand, a rose tendril forgotten between my fingers. His dark eyes bore into mine, carrying an intensity I hadn't seen before. There was an edge to his gaze, a heat that sent a shiver down my spine, instantly warming my cheeks.

For a moment, I forgot about the roses, the unruly garden, and my stubborn commitment to tame it. I was painfully aware of every thorn pressing into my gloves, every bead of sweat trickling down my back, and every breath I drew into my lungs.

But then, just as suddenly as it happened, the moment passed. Heath's stern expression returned, his eyes flicking away dismissively as he moved out of sight, the window being closed behind him.

A moment longer, I stared at the now-closed window, the ghost of his intense gaze still lingering in the air. Then, shaking myself out of my stupor, I forced my attention back to the roses, the untamed climbers seeming far less daunting in comparison.

At least, given Heath's tendency to stay inside the manor house, I didn't have to worry I would bump into him anytime soon.

I was wrong.

The morning air was cool and crisp as I ambled into the manor's kitchen, ready for a small break before returning to tackle the roses.

I poured the boiling water over the tea leaves, the steam curling upwards in a fragrant cloud.

Wrapping my hand around the steaming mug, I inhaled, enjoying the moment of rest - only then Heath marched into the kitchen and stopped as he saw me.

"Ackerley," he said, his voice as cool and measured as ever. As if I haven't just seen him half-naked.

"Thornvale," I responded, my tone matching his. I held his eyes, refusing to be the first to look away.

There was a pause, the silence between us stretching. Finally, he broke it. "Seems like you've been... enjoying the view," he said, a note of arrogance slipping into his voice.

I raised an eyebrow at him, unwilling to give him the satisfaction of blushing or stammering. "If by 'the view' you mean your roses, then yes, I've greatly appreciated them."

He leaned back against the counter, crossing his arms over his chest. "I wasn't referring to the roses."

My heart skipped a beat. The memory flashed vividly in my mind - him in nothing but a towel, his body gleaming in the sunlit room. "I've seen better," I countered, sipping my tea with a feigned nonchalance.

A hint of a smirk played on his lips. "Is that so?"

"Certainly," I said, setting my cup down and meeting his gaze squarely. "Your garden, for instance, has the potential to be a far superior view. If only it weren't so neglected."

His smirk faltered, replaced by his usual stern expression. "Then I suppose you better return to it. Wouldn't want you to miss out on the 'superior view'."

"Indeed," I said, pushing away from the table. But before I turned to leave, I couldn't resist adding, "And, might I suggest investing in some blinds? Unless, of course, you habitually give free peep shows to the unsuspecting public."

His mouth twitched, the corners threatening to lift into a smile. "And here I thought I was giving the new gardener some... motivation."

I chuckled, the sound echoing in the large kitchen. "Maybe you should adjust your expectations. If your aim was to scare the birds off, you might have been successful."

I expected him to revert to his usual cold reply, but Heath laughed instead. It was a rich, deep sound that echoed off the stone walls of the kitchen. It was the first genuine laughter I'd heard from him, and it caught me off guard. There was a warmth to it that I hadn't associated with Heath before, a glimmer of light that softened his usually austere demeanour. He grabbed his steaming coffee, and as he walked past, he leaned towards me and said:

"At least I haven't scared the gardener away," he said, his voice low, husky.

"Not yet." I pointed out.

"Is that a challenge?"

If it involves seeing more of him after showering, then yes.

I didn't say that, of course, instead pushing my chin up to lock my eyes with his. I only smiled, leaving the question unanswered. As I turned to leave, I hadn't anticipated that Heath would move towards the kettle at the exact same moment. We collided gently, his broad chest meeting my shoulder in a soft impact that sent an unexpected jolt through my body.

"Sorry," he murmured, his voice close and lower than before. For a moment, we stood there, the kitchen suddenly too small, the air too heavy.

Time seemed to stretch and warp, the ticking of the kitchen clock the only sound in the heavy silence. I could feel the heat radiating from him, seeping into my skin through the fabric of my clothes. The scent of his soap, leather and charcoal, filled my senses.

Heath cleared his throat, stepping back and giving me space. But the air between us remained charged, a tangible tension that threatened to tip the balance of our carefully constructed banter.

"No harm done," I finally managed to say, forcing a lightness into my voice that I certainly didn't feel. Our eyes met once again, a silent acknowledgement of the moment passing between us.

Something flickered in his gaze, something darker. But then it was gone, replaced by his usual aloof expression. "I'll leave you to your garden," he said, reaching for his coffee and promptly leaving the kitchen.

It's your garden, I wanted to say, but no words left my lips.

I leant over the aisle, my breath heavy, the nerves in my body on fire. We just had a conversation, a conversation about me seeing him barely dressed. We… touched. And yet, it wasn't the strangest thing.

The strangest thing was that Heath Thornvale… laughed.

That thought haunted the entirety of my day.

His laughter echoed in my head as I returned to the cottage, the indigo dusk well on its way. The lights were still in Heath's office. I lingered for a moment before heading back.

With my boots kicked off and my feet tucked beneath me on the sofa, I cradled a bowl of steaming pasta. The scent of basil swirled around me. A soft sigh escaped me as I took my first bite, the simple flavours of olive oil, garlic, and chilli flakes exploding in my mouth.

Leaning back into the plush cushions, I savoured the moment of tranquillity. Outside, the night had closed in, the garden's chaos hidden beneath a blanket of darkness. Here, inside, the world was reduced to Buttons' comforting purrs, the steam rising from my bowl, and the cosy solitude I found myself in.

Safe to say, I couldn't enjoy this solitude for long. My phone buzzed, and Caro's face came on the screen as

I picked up. She was calling to update me that she slept with Alejandro and wasn't sure about Roberto. Portugal was hot, fun, and once again, I felt a pang of annoyance - I could have been there with her.

"Right, what's the gossip on your side?" I told her about the job application. And then...

"I saw Heath," I said, trying to keep my voice casual. "In a towel. Post-shower."

Silence, and then a burst of laughter. "Woah, Jasmine, you're living in some kind of twisted historical romance novel!"

"Shush, Caro," I replied, rolling my eyes, even though she couldn't see me. "It's not like that."

"Really? Because it sounds like Mr. Darcy just had his lake moment, and you were there to witness it!"

"Mr Darcy! Heath is no Mr. Darcy. He's more like... Heathcliff."

"You mean brooding, mysterious, and painfully attractive?"

"I was thinking more along the lines of grumpy, stubborn and annoying."

"I see."

"And the most shocking development is not really me seeing him in a towel, but the fact that we actually had a conversation and he... laughed."

"What a crime," Caro chuckled.

I groaned, running a hand through my hair. "I just don't like... He's complicated. Like a labyrinth in human form. Or maybe like one of those really confusing hedge mazes." I tapped my lips thoughtfully.

"So, you're saying you're lost?" she raised an eyebrow, her smirk growing wider.

"More like trapped," I muttered. "Between his maddening indifference towards the garden and his broodingly charming persona, I don't know whether to hit him with a shovel or, well, hit him with a shovel."

Caro snorted, nearly choking on her latte. "The options are endless, Jasmine. And so versatile."

I couldn't help but laugh. "Alright, alright. But seriously, I will need more than just a pair of gardening gloves and a truckload of patience for this garden—and for Heath."

"Maybe try a chainsaw," Caro suggested, struggling to suppress her giggles. "For the garden, I mean. Though, if you think it'll help with Heath..."

"Carolina!" I exclaimed, laughing. Trust her to make light of my convoluted situation. Because it was exactly that - there was so much tension between us in the morning, and yet, with mid-July approaching fast, Jasper would be back in no time. And then what?

And then my summer of hot sex would commence.

Only… what about Heath?

Nothing about Heath, I told myself. Besides, I didn't even like him.

"Fine, fine," she grinned. "I'm sure you'll figure it out, Jasmine. You always do."

"I'll keep that encouragement in mind. Along with the chainsaw."

With a chuckle, I ended the call, leaning back against the couch. Caro was right. Somehow, I'd figure this out. Or at least, I'd die trying.

Correction: or at least I will hopefully get that job in London.

Chapter 12

Heath must have been having the same client as before - the white Bentley was parked on the driveway, shiny in the morning sun when I left the cottage.

It's so early, though. A client or...?

I quickly decided this thought was veering towards a dangerous territory and needed to be discarded like a weed.

Speaking of weeds, I had work to do.

I was continuing my work on the roses, hoping (or was I?) that I wasn't going to encounter another... unusual window view.

The variety of roses was astounding. As I stepped closer, I found myself mesmerised by the spectacle of colours. Delicate petals in hues of scarlet, soft pink, crisp white, and deep violet were sprinkled throughout the garden.

There were damask roses, their tight clusters of pink petals filling the air with their sweet, intoxicating fragrance. Nearby, a bush of grandiflora roses commanded attention with their majestic blossoms, the vibrant red colour striking against the verdant backdrop.

Glossy leaves framed a bush adorned with white roses, radiant under the sunlight. Not far from them were the stunning yellow roses, their sunny hues reflecting the morning light, their cheerfulness immediately boosting my spirits.

I bent down to admire a particular species – a bourbon rose. Its petals were a breath-taking mix of soft pink and peach, fanning out from a centre glowing with a deeper pink hue. I breathed in its rich, fruity scent, letting the aroma fill my senses.

I stopped for a moment, wondering how amazing it would be to wake up to this view every day. How privileged Heath was - and how he stubbornly didn't see it.

With a sigh, I put on my gardening gloves and got to work.

* * *

I spent my evening with Mrs Butterworth, helping her bake a cake and gossiping with her. I liked my solitary evenings in the cottage, but I was pretty isolated, with nothing really but plants around me, so it was a welcome break. Eventually, the manor's housekeeper left to do the laundry, and I gladly promised to scrub the dishes and get rid of the flour on the worktop. I didn't feel in the mood for calmly reading a book; there was pent-up energy inside me, and I thought about going for a run, but that would probably keep me awake. Instead, clearing the kitchen seemed like a sensible idea.

I was about to leave, the sink empty of dishes and the counters wiped clean when a faint echo drifted down from upstairs. Voices. Murmurs filled with an intimacy only the twilight hours can cultivate.

Curiosity piqued, I wandered over to the window, the soft hum of conversation providing an eerie soundtrack to the night. Outside, the mysterious white Bentley stood on the gravel drive.

Heath had mentioned a 'client.' A vague term. Playing the unwilling detective, I started to connect dots that weren't there or, perhaps, were skilfully hidden. Was this client merely a business acquaintance? Or was there something more lurking beneath the surface? A mystery lover, perhaps? A shiver of something I couldn't name slipped down my spine at the thought.

I blinked, forcing the image of Heath, naked, to the forefront of my mind. His skin was warm, muscles taut. I imagined a stranger's hand running through his hair, a hand that wasn't mine. I imagined her dropping onto her knees, her lips closing around him, tasting him, hard and hot in her mouth. I imagined him whispering her name as he moved in her mouth, that low, commanding voice making her dripping wet…

The sting of jealousy was sharp and unexpected, a visceral response to a scenario that might not even exist.

But worse than that was the burning need in my lower abdomen.

"Jasmine? Are you alright, darling?" Mrs Butterworth popped her head out of the corridor, her hands full of laundry.

"Hm? Me? Oh yes, just leaving," I mumbled, coughing from embarrassment and blinking rapidly. "Goodnight, Mrs B!" I shot up and practically ran towards the cottage.

I needed a glass of cold water and a good thriller to take my mind away from the images that were making me way too horny for my own good.

Garden was my focus.

Not how Heath was spending his evenings.

I climbed into bed with the chill of my nightcap water, doing absolutely nothing to douse the fire in my thoughts. The thriller novel on my bedside, with its dark secrets and twisty plotlines, lay half-read. Not that I had any clue what was happening in it. I fell asleep surprisingly easily, only to wake up drenched in sweat and ridiculously horny on a new morning, with a dream - a sex dream, no less - lingering in my mind.

Each muscular ridge of Heath's nakedness seemed to be etched into my brain, his body a geography of temptation that had no business being in my thoughts. His lips tracing teasing lines of the woman's curves: she was faceless, but her moans sound suspiciously like mine. Heath's hand gripping the fistful of white hair as he plunged himself inside her.

My skin prickled with an unexpected heat.

This had to stop.

Gardening. I had to go back to gardening. And this time, I wouldn't mind some rain to cool me down.

In the late afternoon, my work on the roses was finished. I moved deeper into Thornvale Manor's expansive grounds. The path meandered through the meticulously kept landscape, leading me to my next task - the herb garden.

Upon stepping into the herb garden, the shift was immediate. The sweet scent of roses was replaced with a robust, earthy aroma. It was a comforting scent, one that reminded me of home-cooked meals and the simple pleasure of fresh ingredients.

The gravel path crunched beneath my feet, accompanying my stroll. The late afternoon sun filtered through the tall Manor walls, creating dappled patterns on the vibrant green foliage. Each plant was carefully labelled - probably something that Mrs Butterworth did.

I walked up to a row of basil plants, their leaves a healthy, vibrant green. I plucked a leaf gently, rubbing it between my fingers. The aromatic oils released a pungent scent, bold and refreshing, and instantly reminded me of my favourite Italian dishes.

Next were the tall stalks of rosemary, their needle-like leaves pointing towards the sky. I brushed my hand against them, and their distinctive, piney fragrance wafted up.

Further along were the soft, feathery leaves of dill, the sweet, anise-like aroma mild yet inviting. The chives, with their slender, green shoots, released a mild onion scent when I gently crushed a tip. The sage plants presented their velvety, grey-green leaves.

I decided to pluck some rosemary for dinner, impressed with the state of the herbs. The herb garden was doing the best of the whole grounds, thanks to Mrs Butterworth, who frequently used them for her dinners. *Nothing like your own natural ingredients,* she would say, and I wholeheartedly agreed. But even so, she dreamed about clearing the greenhouse that stood nearby and planting more tomatoes.

I really wanted to add a greenhouse to my workload, but I didn't think I had any time or space to work on it. I pinched my lips together and continued to pick the rosemary. Guilt-ridden by not being able to help fulfil Mrs Butterworth's greenhouse dreams, I decided to pick some more rosemary and bring it to her - a small gift, at least.

I was so lost in the rhythmic task I didn't notice the sound of footsteps approaching until I felt a presence behind me.

I turned to find Heath suddenly standing too close for comfort. His tall frame towered over me, blocking the sun and casting a shadow over the herb garden.

"Ackerley," he said, his voice firm, but there was a strange tinge of softness that I hadn't heard before.

"Thornvale," I responded, my voice steadier than I felt.

"I came to tell you that… There is some budget for this antibacterial treatment for the dahlias. Can you send me the details, and I will get it ordered?"

"Oh," was all I managed for a moment. "Oh. Sorry. I mean, yes, of course. Thank you."

I offered him no smile because I was still annoyed at him. But at least this felt like a small peace offering, and I hoped he felt the gratitude in my voice.

Silence fell amongst us. Heath hesitated, then reached out and gently brushed his fingers against the rosemary in my hand. The unexpected touch sent a shock of awareness through me. I looked up at him.

"This rosemary smells good," he commented, his eyes still firmly on the herb.

"Yeah, it does," I agreed.

His fingers moved from the rosemary to my own hand, his touch lingering for a moment too long. I froze, my heart pounding in my chest. His eyes flicked to mine, and the intensity turned them dark blue, like the deepest night.

The sun was setting, casting a soft orange glow over the herb garden, and the silence was only broken by the distant chirping of birds. Heath's eyes travelled down to my lips and then to my neck, trailing alongside my body. I swallowed hard, heat pooling in my stomach. I was suddenly too aware of my exposed legs and the tight top I was wearing. And of a raw hunger in his eyes.

We stood like that for a moment that seemed to stretch on forever, locked in a tension that made my breath shallow. My mind was a whirl of confusion. This was Heath Thornvale, the same man who set out to sabotage my gardening efforts, and who had showed me nothing but coldness since I'd arrived. The way that he looked at me now was full of a lot of things. But animosity wasn't one of them.

Suddenly, he stepped back, breaking the spell. "I should get going and get that plant thing ordered," he cleared his throat, and before I could thank him again, he turned on his heel, leaving me alone in the herb garden.

I stood there for a while longer, the scent of rosemary strong in the air and the echo of his touch still tingling on my skin. As I resumed my work, I couldn't shake off the feeling that something had shifted between us. Something that made the herb garden feel a lot warmer than it had a few moments ago.

A couple of hours later, I sauntered into the kitchen with an armful of rosemary. The warm air wrapped around me like a gentle hug. As if on cue, Mrs. Butterworth turned around, her rotund figure framed by an apron adorned with the silliest cat print you'd ever seen. A mischievous twinkle shone in her eyes, hidden beneath her fluffy white hair that was always neatly tied back. Parker sat in the corner with a cup of tea, staring down with a scowl. Buttons was sitting on Parker's freshly polished shoes, tail swishing, emerald eyes defiantly staring back at Parker's grimace.

"Hi, Parker and Buttons. Hi, Mrs. B, I brought some rosemary."

"Oh, Jasmine, dear. You're such a gem! Just leave it on the counter, will you?"

Just as I was setting the rosemary on the kitchen counter, Buttons made his next move. With a leap worthy of an Olympic athlete, he landed on the pile of herbs. The cat had decided to explore the fresh rosemary... by rolling all over it.

Mrs. Butterworth and I burst into laughter. Parker growled.

"This infernal creature!"

"Buttons!" I called, scooping the furry culprit off the counter. "Seriously, if you are going to behave like this, I will get on Team Parker in this debacle," I told him. Buttons only swished his tail at me in response.

"Honestly, all of you are causing such a commotion, and I have dinner to prepare!" Mrs Butterworth looked up from the bowl of dough with a mock scolding tone.

She winked at me, flour dusting off her fingers as she waved them at me, sending me into a fit of laughter. "Out with you, child. I have work to do. You too, Parker! And take this insolent cat with you," Parker sighed loudly, reaching for Buttons, who sprinted out of the kitchen.

Laughing, I followed Parker out and said my goodbyes as I slipped through the manor's heavy door.

I stopped in my tracks as soon as I got out. There was that familiar white Bentley. The vehicle hummed to life, pulling away from the manor. I peered towards the windows but couldn't see who the driver was. What I could see, however, was Heath standing on the driveway, his lips pinched tight, his fists clenched tightly.

Taking a deep breath, I made my way towards him.

When Heath turned around, I was taken aback by the hard set of his jaw, and the grim look in his eyes. It was as if all the life had been sucked out of him. He looked tired, older, and burdened.

"Thornvale?" I called out, quickening my pace to reach him. "Are you okay?"

He didn't answer immediately, just stared at the retreating car until it disappeared. Then he let out a long breath.

"I'm fine," he said, finally turning to me. His eyes were hard, but there was an underlying vulnerability that tugged at my heart.

"You don't look fine," I said, studying him. "Who was that?"

His features were inscrutable. "No one who you need to be concerned about," he said, the corners of his mouth twisting into a bitter smile.

I wanted to ask more, to understand what was troubling him. But the guarded look in his eyes told me he wasn't ready to share, and I didn't want to push him. I just nodded, and we stood there in silence, watching the sunset paint the sky with shades of red and gold.

For all the beauty around us, the manor, the gardens, the sunset, all I could think of was the troubled man standing next to me, carrying a weight that he wouldn't - or couldn't - share.

Chapter 13

I didn't see Heath for the next few days, which was probably for the best. I didn't need the distraction with all the work that was going on in the garden. The weather was turning hotter and hotter, with the beginning of July approaching soon - it would mark a month of my battle with the Thornvale Manor's garden.

And I was… impressed. It still didn't look great, admittedly, but the roses were cleared, the dahlias were reacting positively to the antibacterial treatment that arrived a couple of days ago, and the herb garden was doing well. I could see some minor progress, which only fuelled my motivation. Jasper would be returning soon, and I was eager to impress him.

There was also an email that landed in my inbox: an invitation to that job interview for the famous London landscaping company. I have spent the next few evenings outside of the cottage, enjoying the balmy weather and creating some notes to prepare for it. It was scheduled for the first week of July, and I already called my parents, telling them to keep their fingers crossed for me.

When Mrs Butterworth complained she hadn't seen me at breakfast for a while, I decided to join in. On a warm Sunday morning, I put on a floaty, short white dress and marched towards the manor. I was curious whether I would see Heath. Part of me wanted to… okay, no, most of me wanted to. But only because I have been feeling a bit lonely this last week, too preoccupied with interview preparation to have a cup of tea with Mrs Butterworth or a dinner with my parents in town.

So when I saw Heath, a flutter of excitement felt like thousands of butterflies in my stomach.

Only it was soon replaced by the feeling of a weighted awkward silence pressing against my chest. We had barely exchanged a few words since we sat down (typical), and I couldn't help but fidget with my napkin *again*, desperately trying to think of something to say.

"Toast... toast is nice," I said, mentally slapping myself for such a random and uninteresting statement.

Heath looked up at me, confusion etched on his face. "Toast? Yes, I suppose it is," he replied.

I cringed, desperately searching my brain for something more meaningful to say. "Uh, did you know that toast has a magical ability to always land butter-side down when it falls?" I blurted out, realising how ridiculous and unrelated it sounded. Perhaps better no conversation than my painful jokes, I thought, mortified.

But to my surprise, Heath raised an eyebrow, his lips twitching. "Is that so? I guess the laws of gravity have a particular fondness for butter," he responded with a hint of a smile.

I couldn't help but laugh, grateful for his light-hearted response. "It's a scientific phenomenon that has ruined many breakfasts throughout history," I quipped, a giggle escaping my lips.

Heath chuckled. "I'll make sure to watch out for any airborne toast in the future," he said.

"You seem to be enjoying our conversation for once," I commented, emboldened by his amusement.

"What makes you think that?"

"You smiled for once. And you're not rushing back to your office."

Having the final sip of his coffee, he stood up, pausing at the edge of the table.

"And here is where you are wrong, I'm afraid. Have a good day, Ackerley."

"And you, Thornvale. Sorry," I said in mock horror, "*Lord* Thornvale."

"That's better," he smirked before leaning towards me: "You're a fast learner," his low voice made heat pool down in my stomach, and I squeezed my thighs together. He noticed. Pulling back, Heath's dark eyes met mine, gleaming with a hint of playful triumph. He studied me for a moment, an eyebrow arching in amusement, "Seems like I'm not the only one enjoying this conversation."

I swallowed hard. I wasn't enjoying the conversation. I *shouldn't*.

He gave me a final lingering look before disappearing into the belly of the manor. He walked past Mrs Butterworth who just appeared to clear up the table.

"I saw nothing," Mrs Butterworth gave me a knowing smile.

"Yes, exactly, because there was nothing to see," I coughed, trying to mask my embarrassment. "Should I help with clearing up?"

"Oh no, no, you have your own responsibilities," the housekeeper replied.

"Alright then, I should get going," I cleared my throat, blush creeping up my neck.

"Have fun, child," she said, and somehow, I had a suspicion she didn't only mean the garden.

Still, it was the garden that required my attention, and I was getting frustrated with how scattered my brain was today. I forgot a couple of gardening tools and couldn't focus on any job. I blamed the heat.

And Heath Thornvale.

Who said he was enjoying our conversation.

Who made me feel like I wanted him to strip that stupid white dress off me, to push me onto the table. To spread my legs wide open and to drop to his knees, his lips between my legs…

Jasmine Ackerley, I scolded myself internally, partially shocked by my thoughts. And partially wanting my fantasy, undoubtedly brought by unbearable heat that made me delusional, to turn into reality.

Which was why the first thing that I did after finishing my work for the day was head straight for the shower, letting the cold water wash over my body. When

I returned to the kitchen, I saw Caro had tried to call. I dialled her number, seeing her face appearing on the screen.

"Sorry I didn't pick up. I just had a shower," I explained, pointing at my wet hair.

"Because of the heat or Heath?" My best friend grinned.

"Caro," I moaned. "The heat, obviously. Having said that…" I sighed and told her about our conversation in the morning and how he suddenly seemed to care enough for the garden to get me the things I needed.

"Am I sensing a budding desire?" Caro teased.

"You've got to be kidding me," I groaned, making a face at her. "The only thing budding is my desire to whack him with a garden rake."

Caro fell into a fit of laughter, and I had to smile despite my annoyance. Trust her to lighten the mood. "You know, you really have a way with words, Jasmine. Ever considered writing a romantic comedy?"

"I'll take that as a compliment," I said, rolling my eyes. "And who knows? Maybe I'll write one someday based on this summer. I can see the title now: 'Love, Lies, and Landscaping.'"

Caro was still giggling. "With your luck, it would turn into a horror story halfway through. Maybe call it 'When Hedgerows Attack.' Or, 'Nightmare on Elm Tree.'"

"You're having way too much fun with this," I grumbled. But truthfully, I was grateful for her light-hearted banter. It took the edge off the tangled mess that was my garden and, arguably, my life.

As we finished talking, the soft light of dusk descended upon my quaint little cottage. I settled into the sofa, Buttons on my lap. He materalised from nowhere again, and I started to develop this theory that he might have actually been a ghost. The day had drawn to a close, leaving behind the soothing, rhythmic cadence of a gentle rain tapping against the roof and windowpanes. I was glad it was raining - it had been far too hot.

A calm quietness enveloped the cottage, a stark contrast to the day's hustle and bustle. I took some white wine from the fridge, allowing myself an evening without doing interview preparation. My brain felt overloaded as it was. The only sounds were the occasional rustle of the trees, the whispers of rain, and the turning of pages as I dove headfirst into the world of my new book. The rain outside seemed to grow more persistent, creating a soothing backdrop to my cosy evening.

I took a big sip, exhaling slowly. I looked at my book but couldn't focus. My thoughts were constantly bringing me back to the topic of one annoying lord of the manor. I was glad that Heath warmed up to me - it just made my job easier.

But it isn't just about that, is it, Jasmine?

I groaned. Buttons, who escaped to the cottage from the rain, looked up at me. I put my hand on his fluffy head, patting it gently.

No, it wasn't just about the work. I had to admit to myself that I found Heath attractive. Where Jasper was a golden ray of sunshine, easy-going and fun, Heath was a deep, dark night, stormy, yet at the same time soothing. Intriguing.

I told myself a big part of that attraction was the fact that he was practically the only person I would see, apart from Parker and Mrs Butterworth. That it was difficult not to be attracted to him, seeing as he was good looking and in such close proximity to me.

I took another deep breath, returning to my book with a sudden finality.

Jasper Thornvale would be coming back in a few weeks, and that would put an end to all of that nonsense.

The only problem was that I wasn't sure if I wanted it to end.

Ugh.

Chapter 14

The weeks went pleasantly by. With the roses taken care of, I moved on to my next task - the ancient wisteria that clung stubbornly to the crumbling stone wall that marked the boundary of the manor grounds. Its gnarled vines twisted and turned like ancient serpents, heavy with clusters of white blossoms that filled the air with a subtle, sweet scent. Every now and then, a soft breeze would ruffle through its leaves, shaking loose a shower of white petals.

The wisteria, though wildly beautiful, had a mind of its own. The stubborn vines tended to stray, often creeping into the cracks in the stone wall, threatening to tear it down. It was a delicate dance, nurturing the plant while keeping its destructive tendencies at bay. As I trimmed and guided the wisteria, sweat trickling down the back of my neck, I pondered whether I should attend my parent's Summer Solstice party. Mum was from Sweden, and she loved celebrating Midsummer; there was always a party with lots of Swedish and English delicacies.

In the end, I decided against it. There would be lots of my parents' friends around, but not many people my age. With my arms aching from the incessant pruning and training, I thought about having a nice picnic instead. In fact, I had just the right spot for it in mind.

Which was why, as soon as the clock hit seven in the evening, I rummaged through the Thornvale Manor kitchen, remembering Mrs Butterworth encouraging me to help myself to anything I needed.

So armed with my picnic basket — the trove of all my favourite summer goodies — I tread over the sun-kissed carpet of grass, barefoot and adventurous. I loved the feeling of summer grass underneath my feet and found shoes unnecessary. Wearing a short, linen summer dress was nice, too, with the breeze coiling around my bare legs.

My picnic basket swung, matching my stride. It was the longest day of the year, and I was hell-bent on soaking up every second of sunlight. Especially that a few days ago, I discovered this charming, fairytale-like spot, which I was now heading towards. It was on the edge of the garden and woodland, and an ancient oak that presided over the spot like an old king – gnarled, imposing, and wise. Its broad, leaf-laden branches reached out protectively, creating a cool, dappled canopy against the summer solstice sun. Around the base of the oak was a dense throng of roses, creating a velvety moat of crimson and pink. The ground was a bed of daisies and buttercups, basking in the sun like lazy cats. It felt less like a gateway to a picnic spot and more like the wardrobe portal to Narnia. If a white rabbit had hopped by, watch in paw, I wouldn't have been the least bit surprised.

I shook out the chequered blanket, a makeshift stage for my solstice feast, its red and white pattern seeming at odds with the natural hues around me.

From the basket, I got out the ingredients of my banquet: a dog-eared fantasy book whose spine had been bent by a thousand openings, strawberries red as fairytale apples, a Brie that had surrendered to the warmth into a gooey indulgence, and an elderflower cordial. I settled against the oak and bit into strawberry, opening the book and letting a long exhale.

It was a moment straight out of a cliché-ridden novel – a hidden spot in the old garden, a midsummer day, a girl, a picnic. It was as if I had stumbled onto the set of a low-budget indie film. But hey, as far as clichés go, it was a damn good one. I felt my aching muscles relaxing, my mind blissfully escaping into a book about a poor human woman taken into a dangerous but seductive faerie realm with an even more seductive fairy lord.

Before I knew it, the hours had trickled away like a stream, and the sun lingered on the horizon, bathing everything in a rosy glow that gradually faded into twilight. Nightfall may have rolled down its curtain, and I put my book down because I wasn't exactly done.

Inspired by my parents' parties, I got out the LED fairy lights, wrapped them around the sturdy trunk of the old oak, allowed them to drape over the limbs, and they blinked back at me, a thousand twinkling stars brought down to earth. Next were the candles. I drew out an assortment of them from the basket – some tall and slender, others stout and chunky. As I lit them, each flame seemed to dance, painting the surrounding petals with a warm, orange tint. The flickering candles cast shadows that waltzed with the fairy lights, creating a light show that had no business being in a garden but somehow felt perfect. None of them were scented - the night phlox were doing a good enough job of that with its vanilla undertones.

Caro would have a heart attack if she saw that, and drag us into the local pub, but it was a perfect setting for my faerie romance.

Satisfied, I sat back cross-legged on the blanket and returned to my book. Around me, the chorus of the night had begun. The owls took the lead, their hoots echoing in the silence. A symphony of crickets joined in, and a gentle wind rustled the leaves, adding a soft, percussive rhythm.

Literally a perfect summer evening.

But then, just as I was about to bite into another fat, succulent strawberry, a rustling sound snagged my attention. Like the cautious scuffling of a fox or the hushed footsteps of a phantom. I froze, the half-eaten berry poised mid-air. Then, in the twilight, a figure emerged from the surrounding foliage.

Heath Thornvale stepped out of the shadows, looking like some rogue prince from a forgotten fairytale. I knew I had to curb my romantic side at this moment, but it refused to be tamed. His eyes widened in surprise at the sight before him.

"Heath," I said, more surprised than I cared to admit.

"Well, well, Ackerley," he drawled, coming closer, taking in the whole scene – the fairy lights, the candles, the picnic remnants. "Seems like you're having your own private festival. Did I miss the invitation?"

His voice was as smooth and as unwelcome as a summer downpour. I bristled, instantly on the defensive. "No invitation, Thornvale. Just needed a bit of tranquillity. But it looks like that's too much to ask. And besides, it's not a festival."

"What is it, then?"

"My humble fairyland, your Highness," I replied, the sarcasm thick in my voice. I took a sip of my cordial, doing my best impression of not caring, even as my heart fluttered in my chest like a trapped bird.

He took a few steps towards the blanket, his shoes crunching the delicate buttercups underfoot. Sacrilege.

"I must say, it's an interesting spot you have here," he remarked, glancing around at the fairy lights and candles. There was an uncomfortable pause, then, as we both ran out of witty retorts. He moved closer, perhaps drawn by the glow of the fairy lights or the magnetism of awkward silence.

"Is it now?" I shot back. "And here I thought your type would prefer the cold sterility of marble and steel."

His gaze finally fell on me, a pair of blue eyes that looked too icy in the warm glow of the candlelight. A tiny shiver danced its way down my spine. "My 'type'?"

I sipped my cordial, hoping my nonchalance would throw him off balance. "Yes, you know, the 'all-business, no-play' type.'"

A flicker of irritation passed through his eyes, but it quickly disappeared. "And you? The 'live in a fantasy world with fairy lights and imaginary romances' type?"

I choked on my cordial. Imaginary romances? Seriously? "Oh, I'm sorry, are you jealous because your corporate soirées with stuffed-shirt investors can't hold a candle to a simple twilight picnic?"

Heath was now just a couple of feet away, close enough for me to see the quirk of his lips. Was he... amused?

"Never thought I'd see the day where I'd be outdone by fairy lights."

"And yet, here you are," I replied primly. "In *my* secret spot, surrounded by *my* fairy lights. So, if you don't mind," I tapped my book cover, "I'd rather return to my book whilst you're leaving."

He raised an eyebrow. "And if I don't leave?"

"Then you can sit down, shut up and enjoy my midsummer night's dream," I replied, gesturing to the spot beside me on the blanket with an insolence I didn't know I possessed.

His eyebrows shot up, a smirk playing on his lips. "Well, when you put it that way, how could I possibly refuse?"

He folded his tall frame onto the blanket, an arrogant panther joining my picnic. The air around us pulsed with an electric charge, and my tranquil midsummer night suddenly felt like it was on the brink of a storm. And, for some inexplicable reason, I found myself looking forward to the rain.

"I honestly can't believe this," I sighed, unsure what to do next. We weren't exactly friendly. There was no fun conversation to be had.

"And yet," he murmured, stopping just a breath away, his eyes dancing with the same fire as the candles, "here we both are."

Heath's face was flushed, his eyes cold fire, and I did something I never expected to do.

I leaned in to kiss him.

I expected he would pull away. I expected surprise on his part but found none. Heath's hands found my waist, closing the space between us. I felt the hardness of his body against mine when I closed my legs around his hips. His hands travelled up, his thumbs catching on the underside of my breasts. My nipples pinched against my dress, the friction nearly unbearable. He pulled away softly, only to search my face.

"More," I whispered.

He rolled his hips against mine, and my dress hiked up. Slowly, and still slightly hesitant, I put my arms around him and explored the ridges of the muscles on his arms.

"You have no idea how much I wanted to do this," he breathed into my neck, his lips pressed against my earlobe.

"You did?" my eyes widened, and all I could see were stars above me.

He didn't answer; instead, his lips traced my neckline and then my collarbones, hot and fierce. As if he couldn't get enough of me. I pressed my hands against his chest, tugging at it impatiently, wanting to tear it away from him but not being brave enough.

My thighs tightened against his legs as he cupped my breasts. I let out a moan, soft and encouraging, hoping that all the stars above us would listen to my wish and never let him stop touching me.

And then, a sound.

"Buttons!" Parker's angry and not-so-distant voice pierced the night. I pushed Heath away - there was no way I was letting his family butler find us like this.

"We should go," I said breathlessly, even though every nerve in my body burned with yearning to stay.

"Yes," he inhaled, standing up and brushing off his trousers and gestured for me to come with him. I jumped onto my feet, adjusting my dress and scoping most of my belongings into one, incoherent pile. I followed Heath away from the garden, where Parker's voice still boomed in the search of the unruly cat until we were safely on the driveway.

"Goodnight, Ackerley," Heath's smile was shadowed by the deep indigo of the night.

"Goodnight," I whispered back, watching him walk away.

I pressed my hand on the wooden door of the cottage, taking in a deep breath of the cool night air, trying to calm down my shaking body.

And only then I realised that jasmine flowers were now in full bloom.

Chapter 15

I blinked, morning light already streaming through the curtains of Jasmine Cottage. The world outside was all sunshine and birdsong. A perfectly idyllic English summer morning. I, on the other hand, was in utter turmoil.

I drew the quilt up around me as if it could protect me from my thoughts. Heath Thornvale, had kissed me. And the worst part? I thoroughly enjoyed it.

Rolling onto my back, I stared at the wooden beams crisscrossing the ceiling of my cottage. They seemed as knotted and convoluted as my thoughts. The man was a walking contradiction – cold yet warm, distant yet close, frustrating yet... attractive. I rolled over again, burying my face in the pillow as if trying to hide from my own thoughts. But there was no escaping the truth – I was attracted to Heath.

Yes, the same Heath Thornvale who seemed to have graduated from the school of permanent scowls and who made Mr. Darcy look like a ray of bloody sunshine. Him. Oh, and let's not forget: I had a crush on his younger brother, who was coming back to England in two weeks. The younger brother who was also my boss.

So how was I supposed to tell my boss (who was also meant to be my summer fling, let's not forget) that I had kissed his older brother? Not just that, I wanted to continue kissing his older brother. I wanted Heath naked, his body hard and pressed against mine…

I sat up, pushing the quilt away and swinging my legs over the edge of the bed. The wooden floor was cold beneath my feet. Heath Thornvale. Of all the men in England, I had to fall for the one who was as prickly as a rose bush and probably just as romantic.

Making my way to the tiny bathroom, I splashed some water on my face, hoping it would wash away the memory of Heath's hands on my skin, his charcoal and leather scent, his… everything. Because today was a new day, and I was not going to let myself be distracted by some aloof manor lord with a devilish smile and kisses that set my world on fire.

No, today had to be about the garden. The endless, chaotic, stubbornly overgrown garden that was probably laughing at me right now.

"So, you think you can tame me?" It seemed to taunt me. "Just like you thought you could resist Heath Thornvale?"

"Shut up, garden," I muttered, pulling on my gardening gear. It was raining this morning, but despite most of the garden being covered in mud, I didn't mind. I knelt down, feeling the wetness pooling around my knees, and started to plant.

A bead of sweat trickled down my forehead, only to be caught by a rogue strand of hair. I wiped it away with my muddy hand, effectively turning my face into an amateur's attempt at camouflage. I took a handful of the stuff, the earthy smell strong and overpowering, and nestled a tiny seed into it. Great. One down, a thousand to go.

Bees hummed around me, their buzz a constant reminder that I was invading their turf. A ladybug traipsed over my hand with the audacity of a seasoned explorer. I shook it off, earning an indignant buzz from it.

And then I stiffened; I heard rustling in the bushes next to me.

"Hello?" I stood up, peering behind it. There, I spotted Parker, who was staring intently at the path ahead of him.

"Parker, why on earth are you lurking?" I crossed my arms.

"Lurking!" He scoffed. "Just trying to find that blasted cat!" He huffed before disappearing behind the maze. I shook my head, incredulous.

I returned to work, but I kept seeing Parker's silhouette popping in and out of my sight as he marched backwards and forwards. I could see he was getting increasingly worried and agitated with Buttons still missing, so eventually, I put down my shears and joined him.

"I am sure he will come back," I assured him, though actually, I was getting a bit concerned myself, seeing I hadn't seen the cat for nearly a week now.

Parker placed his hands on his hips, scanning the garden.

"I wouldn't want him to get lost, is all." He mumbled. "He is a bit of a link to... before." Sadness passed through his sunburnt face. "For everyone," he added quickly, blinking rapidly.

"I hear you," I said softly. "But I am sure Buttons will be back," I added. "How long has he been with the family?"

"I found him as a kitten," Parker explained. "He was wandering around the woodland, scruffy little thing. Ten years ago it was, and old Lord Thornvale was adamant we should keep him." He pressed his lips together.

"Good choice," I smiled. "Look, I will keep my eyes open and let you know if I see the... damned cat."

"Damned cat, yeah," Parker nodded in agreement, but I could see that he was still worried. "Anyways, thank you, miss. Very kind of you."

"No problem." I watched him strolling back towards the front of the manor, shaking a cat bowl full of biscuits.

Finally, I finished off the work for today and carefully placed my gardening tools back in the shed. I returned to the cottage, opened my laptop to send a confirmation email about the job interview, and there it was: an email from Jasper.

In which he told me he was not coming back until the end of August. He said in his email that he would give me a call to explain and discuss the progress on the garden.

The email was very apologetic, and I replied saying it was all good and that I looked forward to catching up with him. I emailed the new potential London job my availability for the interview.

Finally, I closed my laptop.

I wasn't sure what to make of it. I was disappointed. Disappointed because I was looking forward to catching up with Jasper, whether it would lead to a hook-up or not. Disappointed because I felt like I needed someone on my side, someone who cared about the garden as much as I did, and who was as involved and enthusiastic.

At the same time... part of me was actually relieved. So my life wasn't going to turn into an almighty mess after all, or at least not now. I vowed to focus on the garden, to catch up with Jasper at the end of August and to stay away from Heath, and somehow, the latter didn't exactly feel right.

Because one thing that I craved was more of Heath: his voice, his laughter, his company. His touch.

Shaking my head and letting out a big sigh, I called my best friend.

The minute Caro's face appeared on the laptop screen, I knew she was in for a surprise. Her bright eyes and eager smile reminded me that I was about to drop a major bombshell.

"Jasmine!" she exclaimed as if we hadn't talked just the other day. "What's new in Thornvale? Any more ghost cat encounters?"

I laughed, rolling my eyes. "No, Caro. The ghost cat is still MIA. But... something else has happened."

Her eyebrows arched. "Oh? Do tell."

"Alright," I began, adjusting my laptop to focus on my grinning face, "you might want to sit down for this one."

Caro's image on the screen cocked an eyebrow, "Oh, this sounds juicy. Did you finally uncover Heath's secret dungeon? Omg, wait, is it like a *sex* dungeon?!"

"Hilarious. No," I said, trying to hold back my own smirk, "I kissed him."

"You're joking." Caro's face on my laptop screen was a masterpiece of disbelief as I dropped the bombshell.

"I wish I was." I slouched back against the cottage sofa, nursing my cup of chamomile tea, my face undoubtedly glowing brighter than the midday sun.

"You? And Heath Thornvale?"

"The very same," I admitted, feeling a mischievous grin spread across my face.

"But... but... he's like Heathcliff brooding on the moors, and you're more... well, let's face it, you're more Sound of Music frolicking in the meadows."

I rolled my eyes, chuckling. "Thanks for the vote of confidence, Caro."

She ignored me, her eyes widening with sudden glee. "Was it a passionate, sweep-you-off-your-feet kiss?" She clapped her hands together, practically bouncing in her seat.

"It was... hot. Very hot, actually." I shivered at the memory.

"And what now?"

"What do you mean? I guess we just... I don't know. I need to go back to gardening."

"Honestly, you and that garden," Caro shook her head. "I think you should just go for it. For Heath, I mean, not the garden. It's summer. It's hot. You're hot. He's hot…"

I rolled my eyes. "Don't get too excited. It's not like I'm planning a future with him."

"But a fling, perhaps?" she suggested, waggling her eyebrows.

"No," I shook my head violently. "Remember why I came here? I was supposed to have a fling with his younger brother."

Caro laughed outright. "Oh, right, Jasper, your intended summer romance. I'd say you got a little sidetracked!" Her laughter filled my small cottage. "So, are you going to pursue Jasper now that you've had a taste of Heath?"

"What part of 'I came here for the garden' are you failing to grasp?"

"I'm choosing to ignore it because the other option is way more fun," she admitted with a shrug and a wicked smile.

"You're impossible," I laughed. "And for your information, there's no 'tasting' anyone. One unexpected kiss doesn't mean anything. Jasper... Jasper emailed, actually. He is not coming back in mid-July. No idea why. I suspect it has something to do with this art gallery. He plans to come back at the end of August to check on the garden."

"So he is out of the picture?"

"Sadly," I nodded, strangely not feeling very sad. "Anyway. I need to focus on the garden. And the job application."

"You do that."

"Why did it sound patronising?"

"Because," Caro sighed, "it *was*."

Chapter 16

I hadn't seen Heath for two days; he must have been busy. It suited me well: I could focus on the garden rather than mulling over the inevitable conversation about the kiss.

I was practically finished with the roses: I had one more rose bush to clear before I could tick off this job.

This one was called Deep Secret and had an abundance of buds, each one promising a burst of brilliant red in the coming days. Carefully, I trimmed back the surrounding leaves, giving the tiny buds room to breathe, to grow. A few hours later, I stepped back to admire my work, wiping the sweat off my forehead. The roses looked neater now, rejuvenated.

The phone in my pocket buzzed, and I took off my gardening gloves and frowned, seeing Jasper's phone number on the screen.

I pressed the answer button, taking a deep breath. "Jas!"

"Jas!" I heard his voice and smiled.

"How's Rome treating you?"

"Really good: lots of Aperols, and I even managed to tan, although I do look like a lobster." We both laughed.

"And the situation with the artist and the gallery?"

"Don't even start," he groaned. "Under control now."

"So the gallery is set to open this weekend?"

"It is indeed," I heard a smile in his voice. "Very excited about it. You should come to Rome sometime and visit it."

"I'd love to," I said sincerely.

"But Jas, I have something to tell you." His voice was laced with a strange excitement I couldn't quite place. A flurry of scenarios danced in my head. "What's the matter? Are you okay?"

He laughed. It was a good sound, a reassuring one.

"I'm more than okay, Jasmine. I met someone. Here in Rome."

"Someone?" My voice echoed hollowly in my ears. "As in, 'someone' someone?"

"I guess so," he answered. "Her name's Valentina. It's very early days, so you know… but I thought I would stay in Rome a bit longer."

"Hence, you are not coming back in July." I recalled his email.

"Exactly," he confirmed. "I just thought I would give you a call and speak to you in person tpo update you. But honestly, don't worry. It looks like you have the garden under control, which I knew you would, and of course, please feel free to email me or call me about anything. Besides, I am still planning to come back at the end of August, so we will see each other then. I know I am being flaky, but seriously, my ticket is all booked, so no excuses then."

"Sure," I said. "Sounds good, Jas. Sounds like you are happy."

"It's just a bit of a summer adventure." He said. "Anyways, I hope you're okay and that Heath is not being too annoying."

"He's fine," I replied. "But thanks for calling. I will continue to work on the garden, and hopefully, you can see it all in its glory when you're back in August."

"That's the plan!"

"And in the meantime, enjoy your summer adventure. Or... Would she be the one to make the infamous Jasper Thornvale commit?" I teased. I was completely unsure about how I felt about this revelation, but there was no way I was letting Jasper know that.

"Don't even start," he groaned. "Summer fling sounds much more palatable."

"Typical!" I laughed.

We said our goodbyes, with Jasper promising to bring a fine wine from Italy so we could catch up at the end of August.

When we were reunited that gloomy day in March, even though I told myself otherwise, I felt something. A tug of excitement, a promise of fun, maybe of something more with a man I'd had puppy eyes for a long time.

Therefore, I totally should be annoyed. Especially now that the reason why he wasn't coming back was revealed, and it wasn't anything to do with art gallery problems.

And yet...

Heath's face flashed in my mind, the memory of his hands on my waist, on my thighs, his lips locked on mine with such intensity that even thinking about it sent heat pooling down in my stomach. The only problem was, we hadn't talked about it. I thought about the phone call that interrupted Heath's face and a flash of anger and worry, and the mysterious white Bentley.

What if he thinks it was a mistake?

There was only one way to find out: I had to talk to him.

I waited until late afternoon before entering the manor, my heart thumping in my chest. How should I even start this conversation? With every step, my confidence faltered. He didn't seek me out following the kiss, and perhaps that was a clear enough message...

I turned into the corridor and nearly collided with Heath, who was standing there, examining an old vase.

"Hi," I blurted out, and his eyes snapped to mine, a mixture of feelings crossing his handsome face. "That's nice," I pointed at the vase.

"It is," he agreed, not volunteering any more information.

"Well, you'll be pleased to know that the dahlias are responding well to the antibacterial treatment. It seems we've been able to curb the spread of the disease. With a little more time, they should be back to their former glory," I said proudly, hoping that was a good conversation starter.

"That's great news, Jasmine," Heath replied, his usually stoic face breaking into a smile. It was always rewarding to see the hard edges of his demeanour soften, no matter how fleeting. I opened my mouth, ready to bring up the kiss, when the piercing scream sliced through the quiet of the Thornvale Manor. A chill ran down my spine, and I exchanged a glance with Heath. His playful expression hardened, eyes narrowing in concern.

"That was Mrs. Butterworth," he said, already on his feet.

I followed him as he darted from the room, my heart pounding. We ran down the grand staircase, the laughter and warmth from moments before being replaced with a sinking dread.

The scream had come from the garden. Mrs Butterworth stood near the garden entrance, her hand clasped over her mouth and her face pale. In the dim evening light, I could make out a figure sprawled on the ground, unmoving amongst the foxgloves.

"Parker!" Heath exclaimed. I rushed to the butler's side. Parker was unconscious, his face drained of colour.

"What happened?" Heath asked.

"I don't know," Mrs Butterworth was panting. "I found him like that," she noticed Heath taking his phone out of his pocket. "I have already called for an ambulance. They are a few minutes away."

I knelt beside Parker, my hands shaking as I reached for the man's pulse. It was there, steady but weak.

"I can feel the pulse," I turned to face Heath. His jaw was set, the veins in his neck popping out as he fought to keep his emotions under control. His face was as white as Parker's.

The next few minutes stretched terribly, like gooey mud, dark and heavy. Finally, the sound of the ambulance filled the silence. As the paramedics rushed over, their gear clattering and voices efficient, I stepped back, giving them space to work. Heath moved only when they started to load Parker onto the stretcher.

"I'll follow in the car," Heath said, turning to me and Mrs Butterworth.

"I have already messaged his sister; she should call back shortly."

"Thank you." Heath's voice was strained.

My hand found his for a moment, a squeeze of comfort before he was off, disappearing into the house. A moment later, the roar of an engine filled the air as he followed the flashing lights down the long, winding drive.

"I am going to clean the kitchen," Mrs Butterworth announced. "Care for some tea?"

"Can I join you a little bit later?" I asked, thinking about my job interview, which was about to happen in just under half an hour.

"Of course; come anytime," Mrs Butterworth replied kindly. We parted, and I scurried back to the cottage, frantically putting a nice blouse on and grabbing my notes.

I tried to cram more preparation, but my brain refused to function, numb from worrying. I logged into my online interview, and to my surprise, I relaxed into it. The questions were challenging, but I could talk about something I loved. Still, when the interviewing panel said their goodbyes and I shut down my laptop, I couldn't help but think it was probably disastrous. The interviewers said they would let the candidates know about the outcome by the end of July, which suited me fine.

I tried to occupy myself for the rest of the day by clearing the water in the ponds, but my mind kept circling back to the friendly butler and his health.

Finally, the sound of an engine pulled me from my thoughts. I rushed to the window, pressing my forehead against the cool glass as I watched Heath's car pull in. His figure emerged from the vehicle, his silhouette stiff and weary.

I found myself opening the door of the cottage, drawn to him. Just as I stepped onto the porch, Mrs. Butterworth appeared from the direction of the main house, a shawl wrapped around her shoulders.

"Jasmine," she called, her voice carrying through the crisp night air. "Parker is fine."

My heart dropped with relief, and I blew out a long breath.

"It was sunstroke," Mrs. Butterworth explained, her tone weary but relieved. "He hadn't been drinking enough water."

I nodded, my relief mirrored in her expression. "Thank goodness. Is Heath…?"

"He is fine but a bit shaken. He asked not to be interrupted."

I tried to hide my disappointment.

"Make sense. That must have been hard for him."

"It was. Mostly because…" Mrs Butterworth paused. "It's just been a hard time for all the young Thornvales."

"Why don't you come for a tea, Mrs Butterworth? It's a nice evening; we can sit outside the cottage."

"Sound idea. Tea is always sensible in a crisis, hot weather or otherwise," she agreed. I left her to get comfortable at the small table outside Jasmine Cottage, and I returned promptly, a pot full of Earl Grey between us.

"What a day," Mrs Butterworth sighed. "Parker, the old fool, should have known better."

"We have been having particularly hot days," I pointed out.

"True. I am just glad it wasn't a stroke or something like that. He was complaining of chest pains, and it made me think about the worst." Her voice broke. "Though I suppose it was from too much running after Buttons, rather than anything more sinister. He apparently had all the tests done, and his heart is in great condition. I hope they checked his brain, hot days or not; it was foolish," she said.

"It must have been hard on you," I said gently.

She took a sip of her tea. "Parker and I have been with the Thornvales for so long that we became like a family to each other, too. And then seeing how it affected the young Lord Thornvale…" for a moment, she said nothing. The silence between us was filled with the birds chirping. "It's how he found his father. The old Lord Thornvale collapsed in the garden one day, and when he was taken to the hospital, they found he had cancer. And they found it had spread so much there was nothing they could do."

I looked away, hoping that the tears forming in my eyes wouldn't fall. I thought about my own parents, happy and healthy, and my stomach tightened.

"What a horrible thing to go through."

"It was. It was hard on everyone. Everyone loved Eddie and Margot, you see. They weren't the typical upper-class toffs; they had their quirks and their circle, yes. But they were often in the village, sometimes just to have a quick chat if they weren't heavily involved in the charities and community work. They were kind, generous people. Their children were sweet, all attended our primary, always so polite, even though they could be mischievous at times - but they were children after all! Thornvale Manor was always bustling with activity: children's playdates, Summer Solstice celebrations, village fetes… And then Eddie passed away…" Mrs Butterworth sighed again and brought the tea to her lips.

"Margot and the children were never the same. The first year was the hardest. Young miss Sienna was in boarding school at the time. Everyone thought she would return home, but she didn't and… I can't bear to think about her, lonely and grieving, so far from her family. Jasper was always a sensitive one, and so he escaped into art - and he did it so well that eventually, he ended up travelling around the globe, never returning to the Thornvale Manor. He had his reason, poor soul. Margot was so unwell then… and that meant their eldest, Heath, was left on his own trying to tend to the house and his ailing mother. She drank a lot and became a danger to herself. After she nearly drowned in the river, she finally saw sense. She gave up the bottle but, in the process, gave up Thornvale Manor too. Mistress Margot left for their house in the south of France and has not returned ever since. She barely sees the children anymore, locked in the old house. Sienna is in a law firm in London, Jasper is chasing another art investment in Rome, and Heath… he has never been able to leave. A sad story, really."

"Really sad," I agreed, my eyes falling upon the garden. Mrs Butterworth followed my gaze.

"Which is why I really hope you will be able to bring the garden to its former glory. We all need it. It's been too long."

"I will," I said fiercely, though the promise burned my throat.

Am I actually able to fulfil it?

Chapter 17

The next day, Heath left early to visit Parker - I asked Mrs Butterworth if I could go, but she said Parker would be mortified if we made a commotion and preferred to pretend the accident never happened. No fussing, she said, so I resigned myself to gardening throughout the day and then a fresh bottle of Chardonnay in the evening. I brought the glass outside the cottage alongside my book and made myself comfortable, hoping to get into a new thriller that I bought the other day in Sagebourne's Waterstones.

But as I was reading about the detective in the book and trying to connect the dots, I caught Heath about to get into the manor house and waved enthusiastically. Heath noticed me (it was impossible not to notice me, to be honest, sprawled in front of the cottage) and turned around to come towards me.

"Is Parker okay?" I asked as soon as he was within my reach.

"Yes, he will be out of the hospital today, but I have given him a couple of weeks off. I know it was just dehydration, but still. He should rest."

"Sounds sensible."

"He disagrees."

"Of course he does," my lips quivered in a smile, and Heath's shoulders relaxed. "You can give him my best wishes when you speak to him next and tell him I will keep an eye on Buttons. He has been found, by the way."

"Now that will be a relief," Heath concluded with a ghost of a smile. Silence fell upon us, and I studied him for a moment. He was in his tailored suit pants, but he rolled the sleeves of his shirt, and his features were relaxed.

"Do you... errr, want some wine?" I pointed at the Chardonnay.

"Is it actually wine or some demon's piss posing as wine?" He looked at my cheap supermarket bottle suspiciously.

"You won't find out until you try," I sat back and took a sip from my glass as a challenge before withdrawing to the cottage to bring another glass. Heath had already sat down, staring at the wine as if it was poison.

I poured him some, and clinked my glass with his, "Happy Friday."

"Cheers," he took the smallest sip possible and immediately gave me a disgruntled look. "Definitely demon's piss posing as wine," he gave his judgement.

"It won't kill you," I rolled my eyes.

"It *might*," he seethed.

"It's not that bad," I teased. "You are being dramatic."

"Hardly." And just like that, Heath and I found ourselves sharing a bottle of wine, the evening full of light still despite it being nearly nine o'clock. I wondered whether I should talk to him about the kiss, but the topic somehow turned to our childhood, specifically the summer when Sienna and I decided it was our life's mission to annoy her brothers. Jasper wasn't an easy target because he seemed to enjoy the pranks, but Heath was a teenager at the time, lanky and awkward and wanting nothing to do with his little sister and her friend.

"I barely remember our pranks," I confessed. "I must have been like, what, eight?"

Heath groaned, rolling his eyes. "How could I forget? It was the summer of my discontent, thanks to you two."

I burst out laughing at the exaggerated annoyance in his voice. "Oh, come on, Heath. I am sure we livened up your teenage years."

"Livened up?" Heath chuckled, shaking his head. "You two were relentless. I think I lost a few years of my life dealing with your pranks."

"You know what I do actually remember? Sienna and I are replacing your hair gel with honey," I clutched at my sides as I laughed at the memory.

Heath grimaced; the memory of that sticky mess clearly still vivid. "I had to cut off half my hair, Jasmine. And you two laughed like a pair of hyenas when I came out of the bathroom."

"But your hair looked so shiny!" I defended between fits of laughter, picturing teenage Heath, his usually styled hair turned into a sticky, honey-coated disaster.

"Oh, and the time you switched my cologne with vinegar?" Heath added, finally grinning along. "That was...creative."

"I am surprised your parents wanted me around after all of this," I shook my head.

"Oh, they loved us having friends around," Heath confirmed. The mention of his parents plunged into wistful silence. "So," Heath finally broke it, "Jasper isn't coming back for a while, then."

"New girlfriend, apparently," I swirled my glass. "But it's fine. We can still email about the garden, and he can see the finished thing at the end of August."

"True. Have you been enjoying this job? You can be honest with me; I am not your employer."

"Thankfully," I teased, and he gave me a mock-hurt look. "But yes, I have been. It's been a bit of a mission, I am not going to lie, but I enjoyed every minute of it. It's looking so much better. You should come and have a look," I offered, remembering Mrs Butterworth's words about Heath never wanting to step into the garden after his father's death.

"I should," he said slowly.

"The cottage is great, too," I offered.

"Ah yes, the cottage," he scanned Jasmine Cottage carefully. "Jasper worked hard on it. Hope it's nice inside."

"It is, yes, and... wait, what? You haven't seen the inside?"

"I saw some progress a couple of months ago, but not a finished thing, no."

"Do you want to have a look?"

"Ackerley, are you inviting a suspected vampire into your house?" He said in mock-terror.

"'Suspected' is the keyword here. You haven't melted yet."

"Because there is no sun," he pointed out on the soft, indigo evening.

"Oh dear." I gulped down.

"Quite. If I were you, I'd think carefully about your proposition."

And all that could happen inside the cottage, his suddenly lower, huskier tone of voice seemed to suggest. But no. Nothing would happen because we still haven't talked about the kiss.

I wasn't going to go to bed with Heath Thornvale before we talked about what on earth we are actually doing.

Heath was still looking at me, swirling the wine glass in between his fingers. A corner of his lip curled, and I smirked at him.

"I'd risk it. Come on then, let's have a look."

As we reached the front door, I paused, glancing at Heath. "Prepare yourself, Heath. You're about to witness the unparalleled design sensibility of your brother."

Heath chuckled, folding his arms. "Is that a warning or an invitation?"

"You'll see," I said, pushing open the door.

We both stepped in, and Heath's eyes swept the kitchen and cosy living room, studying the design.

"It's really nice done," he finally passed his judgment, and a note of pride didn't escape my attention.

"It's honestly great," I admitted. "I'll show you around upstairs," I offered, and we climbed the stairs.

I have not just invited Heath Thornvale to my bedroom.

I did. But for the design purposes only.

Heath stood on the threshold of my bedroom, his gaze immediately drawn to the oversized bathtub nestled in the corner, right next to the king-size bed. A bemused smile tugging at the corners of his mouth as he turned to me.

"You have a bathtub in your bedroom?" he asked, one eyebrow raised in an intrigued arch.

"Yes, your brother's idea, I imagine," I replied, trying to keep my tone light despite the blush warming my cheeks.

Heath stepped further into the room, his eyes lingering on the bathtub, the bed, and then finally on me. There was a spark in his eyes, an intensity that set my pulse racing.

"I must admit, it's not the usual setup, is it?" he remarked, his voice dropping an octave, sending a shiver down my spine. "But there's something undeniably... enticing about it."

His words hung heavy in the air with unspoken possibilities. The room suddenly felt too small, too intimate. The bathtub, once a quirky design choice, now seemed like a blatant invitation.

"Well, it's practical," I finally responded. "Imagine having a long, hot bath and then sinking into bed without having to walk through a cold hallway. Pure genius, don't you think?"

Heath's smile widened, his eyes still holding mine captive. "Oh, I can imagine that, Jasmine," he murmured, his voice a low drawl. "I can imagine that very clearly."

The air between us crackled with a charge that was impossible to ignore. And despite every logic screaming at me, I found myself inexplicably drawn into the magnetic pull of Heath's eyes.

His eyes flickered down to my lips before returning to my eyes. "The question is," he said, his voice barely more than a whisper, "can *you* imagine it?"

For a moment, I was lost in his eyes, my breath hitching at the insinuation. And despite the surprise of it all, a small part of me wondered... could I imagine it? Could I picture myself in that bathtub, with Heath standing just where he was now, his eyes filled with the same intense desire?

His hands gripped my waist, and my palm landed on his stomach, taking a handful of his shirt. Our hips collided, and his mouth caught mine roughly. I moaned into his lips, the pressure of his erection on my stomach. He traced the line of my jaw and then my neck with his lips, and I threw my head backwards. His fingers brushed my nipple, too exposed in the soft sports bra that I was still wearing. I push my hands underneath his shirt, the warmth of his skin making my head spinning.

"Heath," I started, unsure what I wanted to say or whether I even wanted to even say it at all. I was breathing heavily and decided not to say anything and just enjoy this moment, but it was too late. Heath had already stepped back.

"I know," he murmured. "This is all getting a bit complicated. I should go."

"Okay," I breathed out, not even bothering to hide my disappointment and followed him down the stairs. He opened the door, and the night breeze came in.

"Would you have dinner with me next Friday?" He suddenly asked his hand on the door.

"Yes. Yes, that sounds good." I replied, surprised.

"Great," he lingered at the doorstep, "goodnight, Ackerley."

"Goodnight, Thornvale."

"*Lord* Thornvale," he reminded, amused. I chuckled, watching him head back out into the night.

Jasper was seeing someone in Rome and wasn't returning to England until the end of August.

I kissed Heath Thornvale. And not just once. I loved every minute of it.

And now I agreed to have dinner with him.

Chapter 18

There was no way I was going to go to sleep after Heath left. So, I did only one thing that seemed sensible.

Decided to use that damned bathtub.

I lit some candles that I found in one of the drawers, letting the shadows dance softly on the walls. I brought the remains of my wine inside and placed it on the bathroom caddy, along with my book. I let the water run, making a mental note to get some bath oils for the future.

I stripped off my clothes and stepped into the bathtub, hoping that the hot water would melt the reminiscence of Heath's words. Otherwise, there would certainly be no sleep for me.

As I sank into the water, I let out a sigh of contentment. It had been a long day. I nestled deeper into the tub, the warm water lapping at my bare shoulders. A gust of evening wind wafted through the open window, bringing with it the delicate scent of jasmine flowers from the garden.

They were now in full bloom, the tiny blossoms dotting the vines like stars against the night sky. Even at night, they refused to let one forget their presence, the scent insinuating itself everywhere. I swear, it's like they were trying to compete with the roses for the title of 'most overpowering scent in the garden'.

And, fine, I had to admit that the scent of jasmine was quite lovely. *Just don't let the bush hear it*, I thought to myself. The last thing I needed was for it to get cocky and invade the rest of the garden.

Still, there was something very comforting about the whole scene that I have created. The scent, the warmth of the water, the flickering candles. They worked together, creating an atmosphere that could almost trick you into believing that life was nothing more than fluffy robes and oversized tubs.

My thoughts wandered, and not surprisingly, they landed on Heath. If I wasn't careful, I could see myself getting used to having him around. And I was excited for our dinner.

But life wasn't a romantic novel. It wasn't all candlelit baths and tall, ruggedly handsome men hiding kind hearts.

There were dirty dishes to wash, bills to pay, and, let's not forget, the hordes of roses that needed pruning.

A laugh bubbled up, mixing with the chorus of chirping crickets outside. Yes, this was my life – a nice mix of romance and reality, of jasmine-scented baths and garden chores. And I actually realised that I wouldn't have it any other way.

A gust of wind blew through the window, ruffling the jasmine blooms, their scent intensifying. Draping an arm over the side of the tub, I closed my eyes and let the heady mix of scents, sounds, and bubbles carry me away.

Bring on the roses, the chores, and the handsome men. I was ready for all of it, with a side of healthy sarcasm and a glass of wine in hand.

* * *

Roses? No, not today.

This week, I had an appointment with the 'wild side' of the garden. The rebellious, free-spirited, and extraordinarily dramatic wildflowers.

Marching towards the chaos of colour that dominated the far side of the garden, I took a deep breath. Sunflowers towered over me like judgemental giraffes, their sunny faces tilted skywards. Marigolds huddled together like gossipy old women, their bitter perfume filling the air. And let's not forget the violets and daisies, tiny but tenacious, spreading like they were planning a garden takeover.

I set down the pail with a thud, squaring my shoulders. "Alright, you botanical anarchists, let's do this."

Despite the absolute lack of discipline amongst these plant renegades, something was endearing about their wildness. They didn't care for rules or order. They were here to live their best life; social norms be damned. Perhaps there was something to learn from them.

The work was... different here. The roses demanded precision, respect, and careful and calculated movements. These guys? It was more like a wrestling match. Tug-of-war with stubborn weeds, a delicate negotiation with space-claiming violets, a tactical distraction of feisty insects.

It would take days to sort of this side of the garden. But on the way back to my cottage this evening, I stopped to look at the roses. There's a unique kind of satisfaction in a job well done, in seeing the fruits of your labour bloom in a riot of colour and fragrance. And as I surveyed the roses, pride welled within me.

To my left, the 'Double Delight' roses were living up to their name. Their creamy white hearts gradually melted into a deep, passionate red at the edges, each petal a piece of art. The bushes were heavy with their blooms, the flowers standing proud and tall amidst the glossy, deep-green leaves.

A little further on, the 'Peace' roses had begun to blossom, their delicate pastel hues painting a portrait of serenity and elegance. Pale yellow at the core with blush pink tips, these roses were a timeless classic. They had a gentle charm about them, an understated elegance that whispered rather than shouted.

I moved along the row, coming to a stop in front of the 'Julia Child' roses. This floribunda variety always brought a smile to my face. Their plump, golden blooms looked like they'd been dusted with sugar, their sweet, liquorice fragrance wafting on the evening breeze. It felt like a burst of sunshine on a cloudy day, an embodiment of joy and cheer.

And, of course, the 'Black Baccara' roses. My absolute showstoppers. They were a striking deep crimson that was almost black, their velvety petals shimmering in the soft light. There was a sense of drama about them, a haunting beauty that I always loved.

I could talk about flowers forever.

By Friday, I was satisfied that taming the wildflowers was going surprisingly well and headed out to the cottage to have a shower and get changed.

For the dinner with Heath, I opted out to wear my short white dress: cute but sexy at the same time. I let my hair loose and touched my face up with a bit of mascara and walked to the Thornvale Manor. It would be just us in the whole manor house today; Parker was still on leave, and Mrs Butterworth took a night off, spending it with her sister.

The scent of roasted garlic and fresh basil filled the grand kitchen. A soft jazz played from a vinyl record, its soothing tone adding to the ambience. The room was bathed in the warm, golden glow of the setting sun, the light dancing off Heath's glossy, raven-black hair. He was currently focused on his task at hand - dicing a plump, ripe tomato. He said hello and pointed at the wine on the aisle before returning to his task.

I leaned against the edge of the granite kitchen island, a half-full glass of Pinot Noir in my hand, watching Heath work. He was all focus, muscles flexing beneath his crisp white shirt as he stirred something in a saucepan, his brow creased in concentration. His tall figure was silhouetted against the warm glow of the stove, the sleek lines of his body accentuated by the soft lighting. His shirt sleeves were rolled up to his elbows, revealing the muscular strength of his forearms. A hint of stubble graced his jawline, further accentuating his masculine charm. The crystal goblet felt cool and soothing against my suddenly heated skin, the scent of merlot mixing with the aromas wafting from the stove.

I watched the play of muscles in his back as he moved, the white dress shirt clinging to him just so. He glanced over at me, the ghost of a smirk tugging at his lips.

"Enjoying the view, Jasmine?" Heath asked, his gaze piercing.

"Immensely," I replied with a languid smile, lifting the wine glass to my lips. The taste of dark berries and spice burst on my tongue, matching the simmering anticipation within me. "Although I must admit, your culinary skills are...distracting."

He chuckled, that low sound of the thunder in the storm echoing through the kitchen and right into me. "Just wait until you see what I can do with this zucchini."

I let out a laugh, shaking my head. "Honestly, Heath, are you trying to charm me with your vegetable innuendos?"

"Is it working?" he shot back, turning to me fully. His eyes raked over me, leaving me feeling both exposed and seen. "And besides," his voice echoed, a teasing grin playing on his lips. "Are you planning to sit there all evening, just drinking my wine?"

A soft chuckle escaped my lips, and I raised an eyebrow. "Do you want me to join you, Heath? Would you like me to handle your… vegetables?"

His eyes flicked to me, the corner of his mouth twitching upwards, before he tossed a cherry tomato my way. I caught it just in time.

He murmured, a suggestive smirk tugging at the corner of his lips. "Well, Jasmine, maybe I should put you to... work. See how well you handle the heat."

His insinuation caused my breath to hitch, anticipation fluttering in my belly like an uncaged bird. The promise in his eyes was intoxicating, headier than any wine.

"I'm looking forward to it, Heath," I responded, my voice barely above a whisper.

Chapter 19

The dinner was delicious, and the conversation was surprisingly flowing. We moved from the dodgy vegetables innuendos to telling each other more about ourselves: Heath telling me about his job in finance, and I went through the tales of my gardening jobs in London. We laughed, and I was happy to see him so relaxed.

"This was amazing," I praised him when I took the last bite of the roasted potato.

"Thank you. I am glad you enjoyed it. Let me clear these, and then should we sit down in the drawing room?" He suggested, taking the plates. I nodded, helping him to bring everything back to the kitchen and loading the dishwasher.

Then, I trailed after Heath into a small, cosy drawing room, its walls lined with framed paintings and weathered books. Unlike the grandeur of the dining room, this room had a warm, intimate feel. It seemed to be one of those places where you could lose hours curled up with a good book, oblivious to the world outside.

The July evening was unseasonably cold, an unexpected chill that had crept into the bones of the manor. I rubbed my bare arms, wishing I had taken a jumper.

Heath turned to look at me, his dark blue shadowed in the low light to an inky blackness of the night. "Let me light the fire," he offered, his tone surprisingly gentle.

"Since when do you know how to light a fire?" I retorted, unable to resist poking at his polished exterior. "Don't you have people for that?"

Heath smiled, a hint of his usual arrogance glinting in his eyes. "Believe it or not, Jasmine, I'm quite capable of looking after myself. Watch and learn."

With an elegance that seemed out of place in such a domestic chore, Heath knelt in front of the fireplace. He arranged the logs with surprising skill before striking a match and tossing it into the hearth. The fire caught immediately, its warmth spreading through the room, painting his face in hues of amber and gold.

Looking away, I focused on the fire, its heat washing over me, a pleasant counter to the chill that had begun to set in. The fire crackled in the hearth, casting a warm, flickering glow around the room, and I sank into the plush couch, glasses of wine in hand, a comfortable silence enveloping us.

"This is lovely," I admitted. Heath stared at the fire before sitting in the chair closest to the door.

"Do you always sit this far away?" I found myself asking, the words slipping out before I could stop them.

The corners of his mouth twitched. "Do you want me to move closer, Jasmine?"

I shrugged, pretending to be nonchalant. "I mean, it is pretty cold. Wouldn't want you to catch a chill."

Heath chuckled, the sound echoing around the room, a warm, rich baritone that sent shivers down my spine. Rising from his chair, he moved to sit beside me on the sofa, his warmth radiating against me. The tension between us spiked, and I held my breath, my heart pounding.

"Better?"

I was about to fire back a witty retort when I caught his heated gaze.

The atmosphere in the room shifted, the teasing banter replaced with a palpable tension.

"I don't know," I whispered. "You tell me."

He only smiled in response before taking a deep breath and taking in the room.

"I think this must be my favourite place in the house. This room... my father and mother used to sit here, just like this," he began, his voice softer than I'd ever heard it. There was a wistful edge to it, a hint of nostalgia that I'd never associated with the usually stoic Heath. "When we were kids, my siblings and I used to creep down from our beds," he continued, a faint smile tugging at his lips. "We would sneak in here, trying to be quiet, but they always knew."

I was entranced, watching as this guarded man unfolded a piece of his past right in front of me. The warmth of the fire between us felt more significant now, a link to a shared memory that he was willingly giving me access to. I was surprised, and too entranced in his story to interrupt.

"They never sent us back to bed," Heath went on. He remained fixed on the dancing flames. "Instead, they'd pull blankets and pillows from the cupboards, right there," he nodded towards a pair of heavy oak doors I hadn't noticed before, "and we would all huddle together on the floor."

His smile grew a bit wider, his eyes unfocused as he lost himself in the memory. "They both read us stories... tales of brave knights and fair maidens, of magical forests and incredible adventures. They had a real talent for making the characters come alive. My mother would read the parts of a dragon, and my father would be the beautiful princess. We would listen, eyes wide open, hanging on to their every word. And we laughed… We laughed so much."

"It sounds beautiful," I smiled at him, and he nodded, taking a sip of his wine.

I was there, in this warm room full of memories, with a man who was so much more than I had initially thought. And for the first time since I'd arrived at Thornvale Manor, I felt like things started to fall into place.

It was a scary thought. I touched Heath's arm and squeezed gently in an attempt to provide some comfort. His lips brushed mine, and I gave myself in to the kiss. It was surprisingly soft, unrushed, slow. His hands framed my face, my body relaxing, molding into his. The undercurrent of desire laced the kiss, but overwhelmingly, there was comfort at the forefront. Intimacy, not just pure lust.

Finally, I pulled away from him, grinning. "If it were a romance novel, we would have been interrupted by Mrs Butterworth, who would just be casually walking in with a tray full of tea and biscuits."

Heath laughed, "Then I am glad she has a day off."

"Exactly, we would want her to be scandalised." I nodded eagerly.

"Hardly," Heath scoffed. "She has witnessed some of the wildest parties that Thornvale Manor has ever seen. Nothing can scandalise Lucy Butterworth."

"Wildest parties? Oh, do tell," I teased. "I am imagining champagne flowing, naked bodies in the moonlight…"

"What filthy, filthy thoughts, Jasmine Ackerley," his lips brushed against my earlobe. "Is that what you are imagining, Jasmine?" His hand traced a line across my thigh.

"I…" my breath hitched. But he withdrew his hand and reached for the wine bottle. I nearly let out a moan of protest.

"I must say, I am enjoying your imagination," he said in a low voice. "Top up?" He asked. I nodded, taking a full glass of wine from him and taking another sip.

I needed to slow down on the wine, I concluded, my body burning.

"Of course, it's not how it was, was it? I am imagining Jasper being the wild one; you were probably holed up in your room, studying or something," His lips twitched.

"Ah, back to your vampire comparisons."

"Well," I answered, playing along with his amusement. "I wouldn't be surprised if you've got a coffin hidden somewhere, probably in the basement."

His laughter rang out again, filling the room. But then his gaze grew intense, the corners of his lips curling into a tantalising smirk.

"Would you like to see where I sleep, Jasmine? So I can prove to you there is no coffin?" he asked, his voice lowering, sending chills of pleasure down into my lower abdomen. His eyes held mine, the shared laughter replaced with an undeniable, simmering heat. The air between us crackled, a tangible wall of electricity that pulled at us like invisible strings.

I knew this was an invitation to finish what we had started. To go further.

And with a sudden clarity, I realised that I wanted that.

"For research purposes only," I said. A slow grin spread across my face as I finished my wine, the liquid courage fuelling my daring response.

He held my eyes, a suggestive smirk tugging at his lips.

"For research purposes only."

"Go on, lead the way," I said, my voice breathless. The room suddenly felt warmer, the intoxicating mixture of wine and desire swirling around us.

I followed Heath up the grand staircase of Thornvale Manor, a symphony of curiosity and nerves humming through me. His hand was warm against my lower back, leading rather than steering, and it sent tingles of awareness skittering along my spine.

He paused in front of an imposing wooden door, his eyes glinting with that same playful arrogance I'd grown accustomed to. With a flourish, he swung it open, and I couldn't help the gasp that slipped free from my lips.

His bedroom was a paradox, just like him - a blend of the Manor's ancient charm with modern sensibilities. Antique furniture, tall, mullioned windows offering views of the moonlit gardens, and a roaring fire casting long, dancing shadows across the plush rug. The bed was massive, dominating the room with its modern frame and luxurious-looking linens. I glanced around, taking in the impressive bookshelves filled with volumes of all shapes and sizes and the large bay window that gave a stunning view of the moonlit Thornvale grounds.

"Well?" he asked, a smirk playing on his lips. "Is it what you expected?"

"It's... better," I replied, impressed by the beautiful room. I turned to face him, my heart pounding in my chest.

His smirk widened into a grin as he closed the distance between us. "A lesson you'll soon learn about me, Jasmine, is that I love to exceed expectations."

"Oh?" I shot back, crossing my arms, "And how do you plan on teaching me that particular lesson?"

He leaned in close, his fingers buried in my hair. His lips brushed my ear as he whispered, "Like this."

My breath stopped for a heartbeat as his hand moved from my hair to the curve of my waist, pulling me closer. Our lips collided, and I tasted him, dark, smoky wine and coffee. I started to work through the buttons of his shirt, but it was hard to focus, with Heath's lips now tracing the line of my jaw.

"You're not helping," I chuckled, a throaty, strange sound that I wasn't familiar with. I had never felt such an overwhelming need. My legs were weak, desire pooling between my thighs, and I rubbed them together, trying to ease it.

"I have no intention to," he responded, his lips brushing against mine in the softest prelude to a kiss before landing on my neck. "I want to taste you. All of you. And I want to take my time with you." His fingers traced my bare thighs. "I want you to focus on you. On how you feel... how I make you feel." My hands trembled on the last button as his finger pressed against my clit. I moaned into his hair before his hand withdrew, and he pulled away with a wicked grin.

"So much teasing," I groaned.

"Trust me, all I want is to rip these clothes off you and take you until you're screaming my name. But… I want to take my time with you even more." There was a hint of a soft smile playing on his lips, and something more than desire flooded me. A different kind of feeling, one that I wasn't able to untangle from anything else just yet.

"At least now," I looked at him beneath my eyelashes, "I can finally get that shirt off you," I pulled it away in one swift motion. Pressing my fingers to his arms and his chest and travelling downwards, I admired the muscle definition. The heat from his body was threatening to smoulder my palms, but I continued until they stopped at his trousers. Leaning closer, I gently bit his lower lip and pressed my hand against his hardness, damning the fabric that was still separating us. I unbuckled his belt, but he stopped me.

"Let me return the favour first," his voice, low and smooth, slid across my body and as he pointed towards my dress. I nodded, letting him stand behind me and unzip it. He was patient, methodical; there was no rush, and I was grateful for this. I wanted every curve, colour, and feeling of this moment etched in my memory forever.

My dress landed at my feet. Slowly, I turned around, ignoring a distant rumble of feeling self-conscious. I cursed myself mentally for not choosing a fancier underwear choice. But I didn't need to; I watched Heath's face, hungry and raw with desire, holding my breath. His eyes were gliding against my body, burning like a midnight fire.

"Jasmine, you are-," he started but paused, his head suddenly flung to the door.

It's the creaking sound that suddenly made my whole body stiffen.

The doors opened, revealing a young woman standing there. We pushed away from each other. She stood in the doorframe; her stunning face carefully composed.

The woman cocked her head, her eyes sweeping across Heath's naked chest and me in my underwear. And then she simply said:

"Ah."

Chapter 20

Heath grabbed his shirt. As soon as he buttoned it up, the woman made a step forward and fell into his arms. My throat tightened, and then I remembered I was standing here in my underwear; I grabbed my dress, pulling it on quickly.

The woman from white Bentley.

Heath's lover.

She was stunning in a white silk jumpsuit and high heels, with clear skin and regal posture.

Bitterness flooded my mouth as I tied my hair into a bun again. How could I be so stupid? How could I, for a second, believe that there was something between us, something more than just a summer fling?

But then the woman let go of Heath and strode towards me, putting her arms around me. She smelled of something expensive: bold amber and spicy pepper.

"Jasmine," she said. I tensed, frowning. How on earth did she know my name? And then suddenly relaxed again when she pulled away, and I saw the familiar sparkling blue of her eyes.

Thornvales' eyes.

"Sienna," I whispered, the recognition hitting me like a wrecking ball.

Her eyes widened. "Don't tell me you didn't recognise me?" I was still speechless, relief flooding through me. "Oh my God, don't tell me you thought I was Heath's... Jasmine!" She started to laugh uncontrollably and then Heath joined in.

"That's not funny," I grumbled, looking at the Thornvales siblings. Now, I could clearly see the resemblance: Sienna had the same sharp cheekbones as Heath and Jasper's full lips, and she was nearly as tall as her brothers.

"Fair enough, the last time you saw me, I was eight," Sienna smiled at me. This was true enough; eight-year-old Sienna had long, dark hair that curled around her back; she was now sporting an elegant bob in the colour of her name. "Anyway, I spoke to Jasper, and he told me you're working here. I was on the way to a client who happens to live in the Cotswolds, so I thought I would pop in for a quick drink and catch up. But..." she smiled lazily at both of us. "Seeing as you are busy..."

"No, no, it would be lovely to catch up," I said quickly, my head spinning from wine and a rollercoaster of emotions.

"Stay over," Heath suggested.

"Oh no," Sienna waved her manicured hand, but under the nonchalance, I heard something harder. "I will take a taxi back and pick up my car early in the morning."

"I can get some snacks and wine going whilst you are catching up?" Heath suggested.

"Sounds good," Sienna agreed, and then all three of us left the bedroom. Sienna and I sat in what I now called a big drawing room whilst Heath disappeared in the kitchen.

I took a moment to collect my thoughts, my heartbeat echoing loudly in the silence of the drawing room. As I glanced over at Sienna, I found her watching me with a knowing smile.

"I see you've been getting to know my brother," she teased.

I raised an eyebrow, sinking into one of the plush armchairs. I was probably blushing furiously, but oh well. "You could say that."

Sienna chuckled. "I don't think I've seen Heath this… happy in a long time. You've certainly brought some life back into this old place."

"Speaking of which," I began, all too happy to change the subject, "the garden's coming along quite well."

"That's wonderful." Sienna smiled. "I have a morning meeting tomorrow with the client, but I will make sure to pop by later in the summer to have a proper look at it. And coming back to Heath… how long have you been guys…?"

I sighed. So much for me trying to change the subject.

"Oh no, we don't… we just… it's just been kissing. I haven't figured out what is going on between us, to be honest." I hesitated. It was strange talking about my feelings, especially to Heath's sister. But Sienna was more than just that; we were friends once. "He's... complicated," I admitted, staring into the dancing flames. "One moment, he's all warmth and charm. The next, he's distant and aloof."

Sienna nodded, her gaze softening. "Heath's always been like that. He puts up walls to protect himself, especially after... Well, you know."

The unspoken loss hung heavily in the air.

"But when he lets those walls down..." I continued, my mind flicking back to our stolen kisses, the warmth of his touch, the depth of his green eyes when he looked at me. "There's a kindness there, a warmth that I just find really... I don't know. My head is full of confusion and wine." I confessed, and Sienna chuckled.

"Fair enough. I just don't want either of you getting hurt. Heath's been having a lot of... one-night stands, shall we say, and for a long time, he has no intention of committing to anyone. It's not that he doesn't want to; he's just been really busy." She sighed. "Which is partially mine and Jasper's fault," she added cryptically. "But like I said, he is my big brother, and seeing him so happy... and we might have lost touch, Jasmine, but you are still my old childhood friend."

"I appreciate that."

"And I appreciate you not throwing me out of the door. I mean, I literally swept here, unannounced, interrupted your ... well, whatever you were doing with my brother, and now grilling you on your feelings and giving you unsolicited advice. You might have liked a younger Sienna, but this older Sienna has been blunt, arrogant and perhaps insensitive."

"Typical Thornvale, then," I grinned, and she laughed. "Don't worry. It's nice to see you, and it's nice to hear your perspective on… things. But how about you, Sienna? If we are on the topic of kissing, and you have been blunt, arrogant and insensitive, allow me the same curiosity."

"I wish I could!" She shook her head ruefully. "Nothing to report. I mean it. Nothing. I just have been busy with work; I am working in a top law firm in London, and it's a non-stop grind. But I enjoy it."

As the door creaked open and Heath returned with a fresh bottle of wine and a tray of snacks, we paused.

"Missed anything?" Heath asked, his gaze flicking between us.

"Just girl talk," Sienna replied, shooting me a knowing glance.

"Why do I have a suspicion that I was the main subject?"

"So full of yourself, brother dearest," Sienna huffed playfully. "Now, let's talk about the garden - Jasmine was saying it's going well?"

Heath nodded, and I launched into a detailed (perhaps too detailed, but let's blame the wine) explanation of all of my gardening endeavours. Sienna was impressed, and then we talked more about Sienna's work until the old grandad clock struck midnight.

"I should go back to the cottage," I finally said. I was enjoying the conversation and the company, but my eyelids felt heavy, and I had to stifle a yawn.

"Let's organise another catch-up," Sienna suggested, rising from her chair and hugging me.

"See you soon, Sienna," I waved at her. "It was great to see you. Bye, Heath," I smiled at him and let them have a bit of a sibling catch-up. I was practically at the door when I realised I left my phone in the small drawing room with the cosy fireplace; I marched back and retrieved it from the sofa.

It was when I walked past that Sienna's voice, hushed and worried, caught my attention. I slowed down, keeping my steps lighter.

"You need to tell her, Heath. She deserves to know." Sienna was saying in a low, concerned voice. "It's not fair, it's deceptive…"

Deceptive.

I didn't hear what Heath replied. I stumbled outside. The world came crashing down on me, the fuzzy, warm feeling replaced by the cold dread.

173

Chapter 21

Which was why I had no intention of just simply getting back to work.

Sienna's car leaving in the morning was what woke me up. The numbness I felt last night was gone, replaced by anger. I threw my clothes on and walked towards the main house.

I paused when I stepped towards Thornvale Manor.

The white Bentley.

Still, I wouldn't let it stop me. Whoever the owner of that car was, I wanted to confront them. I had an inkling that they might somehow be involved in whatever "deception" Sienna was referring to. I realised I cared about Heath enough to not wallow in avoidance. Even if our encounters were just a summer fling.

I was rushing towards the study, intending to talk to Heath about what I overheard the previous night when the low rumble of voices from the other side of the door reached me. Heath was speaking with someone, and the conversation sounded intense.

But before I could think further, the door swung open, and I stumbled into the room, completely off balance. Both men turned to look at me.

"Oh, hello!" I blurted out, feeling my face heat up. "I didn't mean to intrude…"

Heath's eyes widened, but then he quickly recovered, putting on an unreadable mask. "No, Jasmine, you're not intruding. Mr. Bradshaw was just leaving. Mr Bradshaw, meet Jasmine. She's... my partner."

Partner?

Okay, things have escalated quickly.

Mr. Bradshaw, an older man with greying hair and a cunning look in his eyes, extended his hand. "Pleasure to meet you… Jasmine. What a lovely name." Ever thought about becoming a gardener?" There was slyness in his question, and in the corner of my eye, I saw Heath stiffening beside me.

What was going on?

In my flustered state, I took his hand, giving him a weak smile. "Nice to meet you too, Mr. Bradshaw."

"Jasmine was just leaving," Heath said, steering me towards the door with a hand on the small of my back. His touch was unexpectedly warm, sending a tingle up my spine. "Darling, whatever it is, we'll talk about it over dinner, alright?"

Darling? Dinner?

Mr. Bradshaw seemed none the wiser. "Enjoy your evening, you two," he said, smiling smugly. "Pleasure to meet you, Jasmine."

"Likewise," I said, confused, letting Heath lead me outside the door.

As Heath closed the door behind us, I rounded on him. "What the hell, Heath?" I hissed.

"I need to go back there," he said coldly.

He was angry.

Good. Because so was I.

I turned on my heel, leaving him with whoever Mr Bradshaw was.

It was only when I reached the solitude of the cottage that I allowed myself to feel everything. The anger, the desire, the confusion, and the undeniable connection I shared with Heath. I thought about mysterious Mr Bradshaw, about Heath's coldness.

As the minutes turned into hours, I found solace in the silence, in the sanctuary of the cottage. There was no denying the pull between Heath and I, the magnetic attraction that defied logic and reason, given our bad start. And there was also the lingering anger that had yet to be fully resolved. It was a knot that needed to be untangled, a knot made of secrets he refused to tell. I tried to google Mr Bradshaw, but I didn't know his first name, and the internet provided me with an endless options of elderly men called Bradshaw.

I looked out of the window, and my eyes fell on the balcony. There, leaning against the wrought-iron railing, was Heath. He was gazing out into the garden. His usually twinkling hazel eyes shadowed, his brows knitted together. Something about his posture, the way his shoulders slumped, the tension in his jaw set off alarm bells in my mind.

Perhaps this was the moment to finally confront him.

I marched into Thornvale Manor, and after clutching between the corridors, I found the right balcony. I stepped onto it, Heath turning around to face me. Surprise passed through his face, replaced by guilt.

"I am sorry for earlier," he said.

"Apology accepted." He sounded sincere, but I needed more than his apology.

I took a deep breath and leaned against the wrought-iron railing; my eyes drawn to the horizon. The sun was a brilliant orb of molten gold, its edges kissing the world goodnight. Streaks of pink, orange, and purple laced the sky, each one dancing, merging, creating a symphony of colours that was breath-taking.

"The garden looks beautiful like this," Heath murmured behind me.

"Who is Mr Bradshaw?"

"Just a client."

"How come he's the only client I've seen?"

"Plenty of them prefer financial consultations and discussions over the phone. Most of my clients are busy people."

"Don't play games with me, Heath!" I exclaimed and faced him, my patience wearing thin. "I've seen the way you act around this Bradshaw man. You're nervous, edgy. You're not the same confident man I've grown used to."

For a moment, he looked taken aback. But then his mask of indifference slid back into place. "My business dealings are none of your concern," he said firmly.

"But they are my concern!" I countered. "Bradshaw was talking about the manor, wasn't he? Is that it? Is he somehow interested in the Thornvale estate? I'm investing my time and energy into restoring this manor. Your business dealings could affect everything I'm working for!"

"I appreciate your efforts, Jasmine," he responded, his tone flat. "But you were employed to restore this garden, and this matter is out of your hands. That's all."

I felt a wave of frustration washing over me. Why was he being so stubborn? Why wouldn't he let me in, let me help?

With a sigh of resignation, I stepped back. "You know, Heath," I said, my voice trembling with emotion, "In these last weeks you made me think you were different. I thought you cared about this place, about preserving its heritage. But all you seem to care about is your pride."

His eyes hardened, but he said nothing.

Tears pricked my eyes, but I held them back. I refused to let him see me cry. With one last glance at him, I turned on my heel, ready to leave the balcony. His silence echoed in my ears, a bitter confirmation of his unwillingness to let me in, to trust me.

Perhaps I was a fool. Perhaps this was just a summer fling, no strings attached sex, I was simply just a gardener, who's opinion did not matter.

Perhaps there was a time once where I would be okay with that. But I grew fond of both the garden, and the man who owned it.

"Jasmine," his voice was strained, "this is exactly what I am doing. Caring for this place."

I paused. The moment between us stretched, and I finally turned back to face him again.

"Bradshaw. He wants to turn the Manor... into a hotel," Heath finished, his voice barely above a whisper. His eyes searched mine, the dark depths reflecting the pain and uncertainty.

Thornvale Manor... a hotel?

"But... but Thornvale is your home..." I stammered, the shock making it difficult to form coherent sentences.

Heath nodded, his eyes dropping to his hands. "I know, Jasmine. But the costs... the maintenance, the taxes... it's becoming more and more difficult to support. Our parents left all three of us a generous inheritance, and if we were to combine it, it would probably keep the manor going for a while. But I can't ask Sienna and Jasper to do that, not when they want to invest the money differently. It isn't fair. So this... this might be the only

179

option. I am just discussing with him the details of the deal. I didn't want to tell you because one of the things that Bradshaw wants to do is scale down the garden, getting rid of most of it and adding the extension to the building. I called you my partner, because if I disclosed to him that my brother foolishly employed a gardener, Bradshaw might not look at the current deal so favourably."

My mind was racing. Thornvale was more than just a manor house. It was the backdrop to our shared childhood, and throughout the weeks, I had fallen in love with it – or maybe I have always loved, ever since I was little. The thought of its grand halls and enchanting gardens being turned into impersonal hotel spaces... it was too much to bear.

And so was the fact that Heath never disclosed it to me.

"How could you keep this from me, Heath?" I seethed, my voice laced with betrayal. "The hotel developer wants to buy Thornvale Manor... that's something I should have known. And you know what, you're right - I am just a silly gardener. It has nothing to do with me. Except it does: I am pouring my heart into this garden, and you are telling me it could all be destroyed on a hotel developer's whim." I stood in front of Heath, my fists clenched at my sides, anger radiating through every fibre of my being. "I am just so furious at you!"

Heath's arms crossed over his chest; his expression guarded. I could see the conflict in his eyes, a mix of regret and frustration. "Jasmine, I didn't tell you because I thought I could handle it on my own. I didn't want to give you with more worries, given how concerned you were about the state of the garden. I know you care about the estate, but ultimately, this isn't your decision to make, nor your burden to carry."

I scoffed. "Burden me? Heath, this is my home too, at least for the summer! Thornvale Manor means something to me. How could you think I wouldn't want to know?"

His jaw tightened, his gaze locking onto mine. "I made a mistake, okay? I messed up. But this anger... It's not just about the manor, is it?"

The accusation hit me like a punch to the gut. He was right. My anger went beyond Thornvale Manor. It was about him, about the complexity of our relationship, about the way he had turned my world upside down.

I took a step closer to him, my voice wavering. "No, Heath, it's not just about the manor. It's about you, too. You're infuriating and maddening, but damn it, you've really gotten under my skin."

His eyes flickered with a hint of surprise, the tension between us crackling like electricity. "Jasmine…" he started, his voice a low rumble, but I cut him off, unable to hold back any longer.

Conflicting emotions warred within me. I couldn't deny the pull I felt towards him, even in the midst of our heated argument. And as he leaned in, closing the distance between us, I found myself unable to resist it.

Our lips collided in a passionate kiss fuelled by anger, frustration, and a raw desire that had been simmering beneath the surface all this time. It was a clash of emotions, a fusion of heat and need, that consumed us both. The anger that had sparked our argument transformed into a different kind of intensity, igniting a fire between us that threatened to consume everything in its path.

As we kissed, the world around us faded into oblivion, leaving only the heat of our connection. The anger melted away, replaced by a desperate hunger for each other. At that moment, nothing else mattered but the intoxicating sensation of his lips against mine, the way his touch set my skin ablaze, and the undeniable truth that we were bound together, regardless of the challenges that lay ahead.

And yet.

"Wait," I breathed out, dizzy and angry and full of desire. "All of this… I need to think."

Heath stepped aside. "Take all the time you need."

Chapter 22

I entered my cottage with my heart heavy in my chest, my thoughts consumed by a conversation that had left me feeling raw.

As if on cue, Buttons came from nowhere and slipped inside the cottage before I even had a chance to close the door. He looked up at me with his blue eyes, a soft meow escaping his mouth.

"How do you just appear out of nowhere?" I crossed my arms, staring at him. "I honestly think you must be a ghost. That's it. I figured you out."

Buttons hopped onto the counter, his tail swishing in quiet curiosity as I went through the motions of preparing my tea. His presence was a grounding force, a beacon of normalcy in a sea of turmoil. I stroked his soft fur absentmindedly, the simple act bringing a semblance of calm.

Finally, with a steaming cup in hand, I sank onto the sofa, Buttons curling up at my feet.

And then, like a dam breaking, the tears came.

They flowed freely, unchecked, my body shaking with the intensity of my emotions. My hand clenched around the teacup, the ceramic warm against my skin. I let myself feel the hurt, the anger, the heart-wrenching sense of betrayal.

Eventually, I tapped on Caro's name and waited as the video call connected. My best friend's face popped up on the screen, her bright smile lighting up the room. "Hey, Jas! What's going on? You look like you've got some juicy gossip to spill."

I swallowed down my tears. "Oh, Caro, you have no idea. Everything has been just wild over here."

She leaned in closer to the camera. "I guess you are not referring only to the garden."

I snorted. "I wish." I told her about how Heath and I probably would have had sex if not for Sienna's arrival. I told her about how happy Sienna was to see her brother more relaxed and how I overheard her comment. And how I finally confronted him, and he told me about the plan to turn Thornvale Manor into a hotel.

Caro let out a long whistle. "Gosh, can't say I am very surprised. Asset rich, cash poor, no?"

"Clearly," I sighed.

"So this is definitely happening?"

"It seems so. Heath says it appears to be the only option."

"Look, I get that you are angry at him. He should have told you earlier. But it sounds like he really cares, right? So that's good, because not so long ago you thought he was indifferent to the fate of the garden, whilst all this time it sounds he couldn't get attached to it. Which makes sense, if that hotel developer wants to destroy it. Is there something else that you two could think about? Something to stop Bradshaw?"

"Not sure if we are in the mood to work together," I said bitterly.

"Maybe not, but let me put it this way: you care about Thornvale Manor, and so does Heath. You can go back to play enemies or lovers or whatever later, but the reality is the time is ticking. If it's just a matter of details, I'm guessing that the final sale will take place soon."

"And how am I supposed to help? It's not like I have millions stacked under my pillow." I snorted, kind of wishing I had precisely that.

"But you have imagination; you are creative. Remember when we were in high school, and we had to present that science project? We were supposed to create a model of the solar system, but you decided it would be more fun to re-enact the Big Bang instead."

"Oh no," I groaned, the memory flooding back. "That was a disaster."

"But it was creative," she pointed out. "Who else would have thought to use fireworks and a bucket full of glitter to represent the creation of the universe? We may have nearly burned down the science lab, but we got an A for originality and problem-solving. And if everything else fails, you could just channel your inner superhero and swoop in to save the day. 'The Garden Avenger' or 'The Thornvale Tamer'—your choice!"

I burst into laughter, the tension of the situation melting away in the face of Caro's humour. "Oh, I like the sound of 'The Thornvale Tamer.' Perhaps I'll add a cape to my gardening attire."

Caro clapped her hands, her laughter infectious. "Yes! A cape and a pair of gardening gloves, and you'll be unstoppable. No hotel developer will stand a chance!"

We both dissolved into fits of laughter, our conversation evolving into a light-hearted exchange of silly ideas and imaginative scenarios. At that moment, the weight of the situation seemed a little lighter, a little more bearable.

* * *

Still, Heath and I avoided each other expertly for the next week, to Mrs Butterworth's dismay. The end of July, like a flower, was in full bloom, the weather hot, though I hoped for a bit more rain for the plant's sake.

We came face to face on the weekend when Mrs Butterworth commanded us both to help her decorate the dining room for Parker's return. He had been feeling fine now and was eager to return to work.

As soon as I stepped into the dining room, I was assaulted by a riot of colours. Balloons in every shape and size floated around the room, their shiny surfaces reflecting the afternoon light. Apparently, when Mrs. Butterworth said "a few balloons," she really meant "enough to lift the manor off the ground." There was something incredibly ironic about filling a room with balloons for a man who had the general demeanour of a storm cloud. But there I was, stringing up brightly coloured orbs of happiness in the manor's grand dining room for Parker's welcome home party.

In the midst of this balloon wonderland, Heath was wrestling with a particularly stubborn 'Get Well Soon' banner, the annoyance clear on his face. "These damn sticky pads…"

I fumbled with the streamers, my fingers seeming to have lost all dexterity in the face of the impending party. The more I tried to control the fluttering strips, the more they seemed to tangle themselves. On the other side of the room, Heath was having a similar battle with a balloon, the innocent, round thing taking on a mind of its own.

There was an elephant in the room, and it wasn't just the oversized balloon Heath was currently wrestling with. The tension hung heavily, mixing oddly with the scent of latex and old wood. This wasn't the time to talk about the situation with the hotel developer, but the remnants of that night on the balcony were between us like shards of glass.

"You know," she began, her voice carrying a note of motherly wisdom, "when I was young—"

I held up a hand. "Let me guess, you're about to say something deeply profound and slightly cryptic about forgiveness?"

The twinkle in her eyes told me I had hit the nail on the head. She merely shrugged, a small smirk playing on her lips. "Well, I was just going to say that duct tape is good for fixing things. But if the shoe fits, dear…"

I pointed at the balloons. "I need to sort out these. After all, who knows how Parker will react if the balloons aren't inflated to his exact specifications?" I hoped I could divert her attention to a different topic.

Mrs Butterworth sighed. "I dare say I don't think Parker's ever seen a balloon in his life, let alone given a specification."

I frowned. "That's… kind of sad."

"He probably wouldn't want you to feel sad for him, but yes, sadly, he comes from quite a… complicated family. He joined Thornvale Manor when he was sixteen and never left. Each year, we have been trying to celebrate his birthday, but he had none of it. Which is fine, of course, but I thought that this time, I am getting my way. We are having a celebration."

The door creaked. All heads turned to see a shocked Parker standing there. There was a pause and then a round of applause, Parker's cheeks reddening at the attention.

"Parker!" Mrs. Butterworth exclaimed, rushing over to help, but he waved her away.

"All this fuss for an old codger like me?" he grumbled, his eyes scanning the balloon-laden room. But for all his gruffness, I could see the glint of appreciation in his eyes. He looked touched, though I could imagine he'd rather wrestle a bear than admit it.

"Parker! Welcome back," I exclaimed.

"Welcome back, old friend," Heath smiled.

"What was going on when I was away?" He grumbled, clearly keen to take the attention of himself.

"Nothing," Heath and I replied in unison, and Mrs Butterworth snorted in the background.

"Nothing," she sighed knowingly. "Nothing, indeed."

Mrs. Butterworth beamed at him. "Parker, dear, we've missed you. Now, sit down and enjoy the party."

We all gathered around the dining table, littered with a selection of scones and teapots in the centre. As we served ourselves, the room filled with the comforting clatter of cutlery and warm conversation, the earlier tension momentarily forgotten.

Buttons, ever the scene-stealer, was prowling around the room, his tail flicking side to side as he eyed the balloons with a predatory glint in his eyes.

"Don't you dare, cat," Parker warned, catching sight of Buttons.

But Buttons, in all his feline glory, clearly didn't care for Parker's warning. He approached a particularly large balloon, extended a paw, and with a swift jab, the balloon popped. The loud noise caused a moment of stunned silence before Parker caught off guard, nearly jumped out of his seat.

"You blasted creature!" Parker exclaimed, shaking his fist at the triumphant tabby.

The room exploded into laughter.

***

Later, I was sitting outside my cottage. The night sky above was dotted with twinkling stars. In the distance, Thornvale Manor loomed - a majestic and ageless structure. A place that was about to be turned into a hotel because, despite Caro's faith in me, I hadn't found anything that could help to save it. And judging by the light in Heath's office still bright, he wasn't successful either.

I didn't want to think about it. Not after this lovely afternoon we'd had at Parker's party.

I thought instead about how we were this bizarre little gathering - a grumpy butler, an enigmatic housekeeper, a brooding billionaire, a troublesome cat, and me, Jasmine, the inexplicably placed gardener in this puzzle. It was as if someone had tossed us all into a blender and hit the 'chaos' button. Yet somehow, we managed to work together. And not just work together but form a sense of...belonging.

It was an odd feeling, realising you belong somewhere. It's like discovering that the missing puzzle piece was right under your nose all along. But I had to stay professional: my employment would be finishing in six weeks.

I let my eyes fall heavily, enjoying the peaceful evening and the scent of jasmine. I had a great time, filled with scones and laughter, popped balloons and vengeful cats. Ah, yes, nothing screams 'a normal day at the manor' quite like an elderly man having a feud with a cat.

Party…

My eyes snapped open.

And then I had it. I had an idea how to save Thornvale Manor.

The only problem was, I needed Heath's help.

Chapter 23

All of my complicated feelings were forgotten in the morning. I was so excited to tell Heath about my idea that I didn't even bother to get dressed after waking up. Instead, I stepped out into the morning wearing just my silk robe, a birthday present from my mum. The cool touch of the dewy grass beneath my bare feet sent a shiver through me, grounding me to the earth. Soft morning light was casting long, artistic shadows over the sculptures and trellises.

The golden rays of the morning sun diffused through the delicate petals of roses, hydrangeas, and lilies, highlighting the dew drops clinging to their surfaces like precious jewels. Blooms bobbed gently on the breeze, releasing their soft perfume into the air. It was a scent I had come to associate with home: sweet yet balanced by the earthy undertone of the manicured greenery.

Walking into the study, I was greeted by the sight of Heath engrossed in his work. His brow was furrowed in concentration as he scanned over blueprints and notes, pencil poised over a document.

"Thornvale," I said, my voice firm.

He looked up from his work, irritation flitting briefly across his handsome features before being replaced by a look of mild surprise.

"Jasmine," he stood up, rushing towards me. "I am so sorry. I should have told you earlier."

"It's okay," my voice softened. "I thought about it and… I understand why you did it. I also shouldn't have expected to know – it is your home after all, not mine, no matter how attached I have grown to it." My eyes swept throught the papers on his desk. "Tell me you are still thinking you will find a way of not selling Thornvale Manor."

He was silent for a couple of heartbeats.

"I have thought I could turn the tide and save this place, Jasmine, I really did. But after yesterday's meeting… I doubt it can happen. I investigated loans, and my siblings offered to give their inheritance away, but it would only last for a few years. And after that?" he shook his head. "The reality is that without a steady stream of income, we can't support the estate. I tried…" he clenched his fists, shadows crossing his face.

"I am sorry. I can't imagine how hard everything was for you. Sienna is busy in London, Jasper in Rome, and you were left alone with all of this."

"I can deal with it," his voice hardened.

"I know you can. And I am happy to help."

"That's kind of you," his voice softened, "but I have already drafted a sale contract with Bradshaw. There are just a few details to finalise, and we are due to sign the sale in the first week of September."

First week of September. I swallowed hard. Not a lot of time left, but I was determined.

"I have an idea," I declared.

He frowned, looking up at me with scepticism. "Don't you think I thought about everything?"

"You're insufferable at times," I scolded him. "Just let me speak. I had a thought about what you said: Thornvale Manor needs to work for itself, needs a steady stream of income. So how about opening the gardens to the public and charging a fee? Not every day; it could be a weekend thing. You could also have weddings and parties in the garden. It would be perfect for it."

"It did cross my mind early on, but… I don't know. I guess we didn't have the garden restored then, and I thought… this wasn't the right place for a wedding."

"But now you do," I said triumphantly.

"I guess I would be an idiot if I didn't at least try."

"Exactly. I was thinking about having a garden party for all of the community members of Sagebourne, a formal reopening of the Thornvale Manor gardens at the end of August. My friend from London, Laura, works as a photographer and has a large following on Instagram, so I am sure she would promote it for us."

"Okay," Heath exhaled, and I could see his brain working overtime. "Okay, yes, that could work."

"There is a teeny-tiny issue, though," I bit my lip. "Okay, it's, in fact, a big problem. I don't think I can get the garden up to speed by the end of August. It's looking much better, but the level of neglect was bigger than I previously expected. Which means that if we want to make this party happen, I need help."

"We can employ more gardeners," Heath suggested slowly.

"We can, but it will take time to get the right ones and then to bring them up to speed. What I am trying to say is: how about you come to help me in the garden?" I suggested, leaning against a dusty bookshelf. A breeze swept in through the window, making the thin fabric of my robe flutter around my legs, the morning chill causing goosebumps to erupt on my skin. His gaze flickered, and my body immediately heated under his eyes, instantly forgetting the coolness of the wind.

He laughed, the sound echoing through the room. "Garden? Do I look like someone who enjoys playing in the dirt?"

"You could use some sun, Heath. You're beginning to resemble a character in one of those ghost stories about old manors," I teased.

"Are you saying I look like a ghost or that I'm haunting my own house?" He asked, feigning horror.

"Both," I shot back, enjoying the banter. "There's more to life than these old papers and ledgers, you know."

"Really, Jasmine? I'd rather be a well-read ghost than a sunburnt gardener," he retorted, a smirk tugging at the corners of his mouth.

"I bet you couldn't handle a day's work in the garden," I challenged, crossing my arms.

"Is that a dare, Miss Ackerley?"

"It's an invitation, Mr. Thornvale. One that might save you from becoming part of the manor's spooky lore."

His laughter filled the room once more. "You're incorrigible, you know that?"

"And you're as stubborn as these old books. So, do we have a deal?"

"Only if you promise to stop comparing me to spectral entities and ancient literature."

"I make no promises, Heath. But I can offer you a chance to swap these dusty tomes for some fresh air and sunshine."

He sighed, closing the ledger with a thump. "Fine, but only because I can't resist a good dare."

"Excellent! You won't regret it, Heath," I said, my heart unexpectedly light.

"I'm already starting to," he grumbled, but his eyes were laughing. "Are we okay, then?"

"We are."

Then Heath stood up. He towered over me, his presence enveloping me in a warm embrace. My heart pounded in my chest, the proximity bringing an unexpected flush to my cheeks.

"Oh, and Jasmine," he added, a playful smirk tugging at the corner of his lips. He leaned down, his breath warm against my ear, making me shiver. "If all you're going to wear is just this robe, feel free to interrupt me as often as you'd like."

The unexpected comment sent a rush of heat through me. I wanted nothing more than to let him get rid of the robe and take me right here, on his desk.

But… we were on a mission.

I pulled my robe tighter and gave him a sideways look. "We'll start tomorrow."

* * *

Heath was waiting for me in the garden at eight o'clock the next morning. He was wearing shorts and a white linen shirt with sleeves rolled up. My eyes lingered on the muscles for a little bit too long and I gulp down the balmy morning air.

"Ready?" I smiled at him, but he didn't smile back. Instead, his eyes were fixated on the entrance to the garden, something akin to concern

At once, I remember what Mrs Butterworth said: how Eddie Thornvale collapsed in the garden, how Heath found him and how it was just a horrific start to his last moments with his dad.

Then, with a deep breath, Heath took a step forward. His shoes crunched against the gravel path, the sound echoing through the still air. I watched him, his figure rigid against the backdrop of the garden. As he stepped into the garden, his steps were hesitant, uncertain. I glanced at him, noting the way his eyes scanned the area as if he were seeing it for the first time.

He turned to me, his face unreadable. "You know, this is the first time I've been here since...since my dad passed away. I found him here. He collapsed when he was attending to the garden, and when we took him to the hospital, that's when we found out he had cancer. And that it's terminal." He sighed, running a hand through his hair. "He loved this place. Spent hours tending to the plants, and talking about the different species. I just...I just couldn't bring myself to come here after he was gone. In a way, I hated this place. It was just a constant reminder of what happened."

I heard this story before, but didn't interrupt, the impact of it far heavier than when Mrs Butterworth told it. Heath's voice broke slightly in the last sentence, and I felt my heart ache for him. To lose a parent was painful enough, but to be reminded of that loss every day must have been unbearable.

"That's why I was so angry at Jasper when he just casually announced he employed a gardener. It was easier for him to escape to Rome and get himself lost in art. I don't blame him, though. However now, I think it's time to start enjoying the garden again," he said, a determined look in his eyes. "Dad would have wanted that."

I smiled softly in response and then led him into the garden. Heath's handsome features were a violent mix of emotions: sadness but also something akin to joy. Perhaps he recalled the memories of his family enjoying the garden, beautiful and taken care of, not the neglected thing that I saw when I first stepped into the Thornvale estate.

"Are you okay?" I squeezed his arm gently. He nodded.

"So," he surveyed the garden, determination filling his expression. "Tell me what needs to be done."

"The garden definitely looks much better now," I pointed at the roses, the wildflowers, and the herb garden. "I have cleared and pruned the flowers and weeded the pathways, so it's nice and clean."

"This is a really good job," he seemed impressed, and my heart swelled with pride.

"But there is still much to do," I began, gesturing towards a set of shrubs shaped into spirals and cones, "in a Jacobean garden, it's all about symmetry, structure, and a certain level of formality. We have the parterre de broderie there and the knot gardens there." I pointed out the different aspects of the garden, the tightly clipped hedges, the geometric flower beds and the water features, all designed in a way to bring order to the chaos of nature.

Heath nodded, following my gaze, "Alright, I get it. But where do I fit in?"

"Well, since you've so graciously offered to help," I said, smirking at his groan, "I thought you could help me with the topiaries. It's time for their trim, and while it's a meticulous job, it's not particularly complicated. You just have to follow the existing shapes."

"Sounds doable."

"It would just add to that feeling of the garden being well taken care of, elegant and neat," I explained and showed him how to hold the shears, how to move his hands to achieve the right curves and angles, and how to step back frequently to ensure the shape was consistent.

The rest of the morning passed in a similar fashion, with me guiding Heath through the art of maintaining a Jacobean garden. It was a new experience, sharing my passion with him. It felt nice having someone to share the load and the laughter.

By the afternoon, I was confident Heath was prepared to work by himself, and I moved to cleaning the statues in the ponds. Parker had already drained them, and I hoped I could restore them to their former glory.

"Heath Thornvale helping with the garden. I never thought I'd see the day," I commented, my eyes lingering on him a moment longer before I busied myself with my own set of garden shears. Heath paused, straightening up and looking at me, a quizzical expression on his face. "See what day, Jasmine?"

"The day you'd finally escape your crypt and venture out in the daylight," I replied, flashing him a teasing grin. "I honestly had this hypothesis you were a vampire, forever holed up in your office, but you sure seem to be enjoying the sunlight," my voice was laced with amusement.

Heath looked up from his task, his green eyes sparkling with humour. "What can I say, Jasmine," he replied with a cocky grin. "Even a vampire needs to bask in the sun once in a while."

I laughed at his response, enjoying the banter. "I hope you have your sunscreen on. I'd hate for you to turn into dust."

Heath chuckled, his laughter rich and contagious. He wiped his brow with the back of his hand, his muscles flexing in the process. "No chance of that," he retorted. "Vampires like me have adapted to the modern world. But, if you're worried, you're more than welcome to check for any signs of burning."

His voice suddenly went lower, turning the seemingly innocent suggestion into a provocative invitation. My breath hitched, the sexual tension wrapping around us like a tangible entity.

"Well," I said, striving to keep my voice steady as I sauntered over to him, "I don't suppose it would hurt to make sure. Don't want you turning to ash under my charge."

The corner of his mouth twitched upwards, his eyes never leaving mine. Taking a cautious step forward, I reached up, my hand hovering just shy of his skin. The moment felt oddly intimate despite the light-hearted banter that had led us here. As if sensing my hesitation, Heath stepped closer, his skin surprisingly warm beneath my palm.

"No signs of burning," I announced, my voice barely above a whisper. His proximity had done strange things to my heart rate. I quickly withdrew my hand, putting a safe distance between us.

A low chuckle rumbled in Heath's chest. "Glad to hear that. But you know what's threatening to burn me alive? The sexual tension between us."

I agreed. "Then we better get back to work."

"What kind of work?"

"The gardening," I brushed off his innuendo, even though it wasn't the thought of gardening that currently occupied my head space.

Only it should, because we had Mr Bradshaw breathing down our necks with his sale.

I left him with the topiaries before moving to a different part of the garden. I myself was close to turning into dust just from a sheer need to rip his clothes off and let him have me here, in the garden.

We met again later in the evening (working in a safe distance apart), when I announced it was time to finish for the day.

"Good work today," I praised him. I was seriously impressed.

"Thank you," he smiled back. We lingered at the entrance to the maze, now looking much better thanks to Heath's hard work. "I actually used to help Dad in the garden when I was younger. I guess I picked up a skill or two."

"Looks like it," I smiled. Silence enveloped us, broken only by the chirping of the birds and the trees rustling with the evening breeze.

"I am sorry, too," I said suddenly. "I shouldn't judge you. You were doing the best that you could, and I don't think it's fair for me to have expected to be told what is going on. I was so high and mighty and thought only about my job going to waste, but I didn't think… I didn't think how you must have been feeling. How horrible the threat of losing a home full of memories is. I shouldn't have gotten so angry."

"You did it because you cared."

"So did you."

"Thank you for being understanding. Anyway, I should head back in; I have some more work to do," Heath finally said. But he didn't move. Instead, he looked at me, his eyes intense, and before I could react, he leaned in.

His hand cupped the side of my face, his thumb gently caressing my cheek as his eyes searched mine.

His lips brushed against my cheek, soft and warm, lingering for a moment longer than necessary.

The world seemed to slow down as he closed the gap between us. His lips brushed against mine, sending a shockwave of warmth through me. The kiss was gentle, tender, and held a depth of feeling that took me by surprise. His lips were soft yet insistent, their warmth seeping into me, leaving me breathless.

He pulled back slowly, his eyes still closed, a soft sigh escaping his lips. When he finally opened his eyes, they held a warmth that mirrored the lingering sensation of his lips against mine.

"Is that how we should be saying goodbye from now on?" I asked, smiling.

"Yes."

"Then it might become my favourite time of the day."

"That makes the two of us."

I watched him walk back to the manor, smiling. He stopped by the hydrangea bush, his fingers gently touching the snow-white petals. And then, he approached the back of the manor and reappeared again, this time with the watering hose. He opened it up, watering the plant with a methodical precision.

The white hydrangeas.

Suddenly, I remember how he told me to be careful about them, how they were the only plants that appeared to be maintained…

And then I understood.

It was Heath who looked after them this whole time.

Chapter 24

If someone had told me a few weeks ago that Heath Thornvale, the reserved, and I dare say, slightly intimidating lord of Thornvale Manor, would be my gardening partner, I would have laughed in their face.

Our gardening days started with the first rays of sunlight, its golden glow illuminating the manor and casting long shadows in the garden. Heath would be there, waiting, the edges of his normally polished appearance slightly ruffled, his hands already bearing traces of the day's work. Because these moments, immersed in nature beside Heath, were becoming my favourite part of the day.

I focused on the herb garden first, sawing more of basil, coriander, fennel and dill. Mrs Butterworth was doing an excellent job with it, but part of my grand plan of getting some stream of income for Thornvale Manor was to sell the herbs as well - which meant we needed serious quantities of them. Sadly, despite the antibacterial treatment, the dahlias were still struggling, so I decided to plant more bulbs. I also cleared the greenhouse and started to plant some beets, carrots, radishes and broccolis so they could be ready for the late autumn harvest.

Heath, on the other hand, took upon him helping restore arbours and pergolas and taming the honeysuckle that was entwined around them, creating a sweet-scented shaded space. After I cleared the water features, Heath helped to install a functioning water system and replaced the benches that we scattered around the garden. He also took it upon himself to sort out wooden and iron wrought trellis to support the abundant roses.

But it wasn't just us two involved. Saving Thornvale Manor quickly became a teamwork. Mrs Butterworth and Parker were involved, too. We set the date for the garden party for the 28th of August - the Sunday before Bank Holiday Monday. I spoke to Jasper, who took it upon himself to organise drinks and nibbles. Heath talked to Sienna, who arranged the posters that I could place around Sagebourne and organised a website designer who would place all the details about Thornvale Garden on the web.

Mrs Butterworth was busy creating recipes for the party. She decided it would be rose-themed, given how much of a pride the Thornvale Manor roses were. She kept her recipes closely guarded - all we knew was that Thornvale Manor kitchen became a serious factory for rose jam that smelled and tasted delicious.

Parker took on restoring the garden's wooden pavilion, rotten and destroyed in the weather. I thought I could plant some climbing roses, and it would make a stunning backdrop for exchanging the vows.

The posters came in early in the second week of August, giving me time to place them around Sagebourne. Sienna did a beautiful job: they were cheerful, colourful and very clearly stated all the information. I rushed to the village and started to put them around.

Soon enough, a young couple approached me, their eyes drawn to the poster in my hands. "We've heard about the garden restoration," the woman said. "Can't wait to see it for ourselves."

I smiled, thrilled to see the growing interest. "You won't be disappointed. Thornvale Manor's gardens have been literally transformed." They exchanged a glance, their excitement mirrored in each other's eyes.

"We'll definitely be there," the man said, determined.

"And I will ask my parents who live in Reading to come over too," the young woman promised.

"Thank you!" I grinned, happy.

With each poster I hung, the anticipation grew within me. This garden party wasn't just about showcasing the beauty we had created; it was about bringing the community together, too.

As the final poster was secured, I stepped back, admiring the colourful display adorning the lampposts. Thornvale Manor's garden party was poised to be an event that would breathe new life into a neglected space.

With a sense of fulfilment and hope, I turned and made my way back towards Thornvale Manor. Heath offered to give me a ride, but I didn't mind a walk. My mind was a swarming beehive, the thoughts warm as the height of summer.

I expected frowns and cynicism from the people of Sagebourne, but everyone seemed so excited. The countdown has begun, and soon, the gates will open to welcome the community. We now had a real chance to save Thornvale Manor from the clutches of a heartless developer. I couldn't wait to tell Heath about it.

* * *

The sweet scent of the honeysuckle flowers filled the air, mingling with the earthy fragrance of the garden. Heath and I had claimed this spot as our unofficial meeting place, where we would take a breather from work and discuss our plans for the upcoming garden party. We settled there now, too.

"Heath," I started, excitement spilling from me. "Literally everyone's talking about the garden party. The villagers are practically planning their outfits."

A smile curled up on his face. "That's good," he replied, and I nodded enthusiastically. Suddenly he frowned. "I actually have an idea. What if we invited the locals to sell their homegrown produce at the party? It could be a fantastic way to promote local goods and make everyone feel involved."

"Yes!" I exclaimed. "This is a fantastic idea!"

Heath's brow furrowed in thought. "Who will convince them, though? We need a negotiator."

"Well," I said, prodding him playfully in the side, "I nominate the Lord Thornvale himself."

He looked at me like I'd grown a second head. "Me? But, Jasmine... I've barely interacted with the villagers. I've been so... reclusive. Would they even listen to me? You said it yourself: I've been living like a vampire in a daytime soap opera."

His vulnerability touched me. Here was Heath, the seemingly invincible lord of Thornvale Manor, unsure and anxious about connecting with his community. But reminiscent of Mrs Butterworth's story, I understood his apprehension. All of the Thornvale siblings, shattered by their dad's death, decided to withdraw from the community.

"Heath," I said gently, "You've been working tirelessly to restore this garden, not just for the manor, but for everyone. It's time they see that side of you, the one that cares about this place and the people who call it home. Trust me, they'll respond. All you have to do is try. And you know what? I'll help."

There was silence as he mulled over my words, and I could see the resolve slowly forming in his eyes. He looked at me, his gaze steady and determined. "Alright, Jasmine. Let's do this together."

As the evening descended around us, the soft hum of bees and the scent of honeysuckle hanging in the air, I felt a shift. Like we were on the edge of something exciting, something more than just botany warfare.

My parents jumped into the occasion of helping and were happy to provide us with the local business owners who could offer their produce for sale. We looked at the list and created a plan of who to approach and when, scheduling meetings.

Which was how I found myself in cosy kitchens, discussing the subtleties of strawberry jam, arguing the merits of free-range eggs over factory-farmed, and debating the correct way to bake a Victoria sponge (it's all in the folding technique, by the way). There was Mr. Henderson, a retired sea captain and now the village's unofficial beekeeping czar. He had initially scoffed at our idea, but after a riveting conversation about the fascinating social hierarchy of bee colonies, he agreed to showcase his honey, which, I might add, had the consistency of liquid gold and the taste of summer sunshine.

Then, there was the Fletcher family, local dairy farmers with a lineage that went back centuries. Mrs. Fletcher, a stout woman with a soft spot for Heath's flattery, agreed to bring her award-winning cheddar and soft Brie to the party, while her husband, a man of few words, promised fresh milk and cream. From reassuring young Timmy that his oversized zucchinis were not freaks of nature but instead a testament to his green thumb to convincing gruff old Mr. Douglas that his fiercely strong homemade cider was just the kind of local flavour we needed at the party.

Heath proved to be quite the negotiator. For all his brooding mystery, he could charm even the most stubborn villager. He stood tall in their doorways, patiently listening to old farming tales and nodding thoughtfully at the merits of homegrown potatoes over store-bought ones. Whilst I was more of a talkative social butterfly, Heath had the calming, soothing presence that seemed to work on the Sagebourne locals, which meant that we ended up with an amazing collection of the produce on offer for our garden party.

It was Thursday, and there were only twenty days left until the garden party. I decided to have a look at all the progress and note down what else needed to be worked on.

I stepped outside, the crunch of gravel beneath my feet punctuating the tranquillity of the late afternoon. From the corner of my eye, I caught a movement - a familiar figure hunched over one of the flower beds.

Heath.

He was deeply engrossed, his forehead furrowed in concentration as he worked in the garden. His sleeves were rolled up, revealing his tanned arms speckled with dirt. A smudge of soil adorned his cheek, making him look boyish and incredibly endearing. The sight brought a smile to my lips. He looked so at home amidst the blooms and foliage, so different from the withdrawn man I'd first met.

I stood there, watching him admiring the view. The muscles in his back flexed with each movement, hinting at a quiet strength. The sun's rays caught his hair, turning it into a tousled halo of light.

Heath finally straightened, wiping sweat from his brow with the back of his hand. The sight was strangely appealing, this rugged, earthy side of him, and it did funny things to my stomach.

"You seem to be enjoying the view, Jasmine," Heath said, a teasing smile on his lips. He'd caught me staring, and the amusement in his eyes was undeniable.

"I'm just admiring the roses," I retorted, attempting to steer the conversation back into safe territory.

"Is that so?" he asked, raising an eyebrow. "And here I was thinking I'm the one making you blush like one."

"You are too arrogant for your own good."

"Don't tell me you don't like it."

"Focus!" I laughed, swatting his arm. "Right, I am going to check on what else needs our attention," I explained.

"Not before this," he pulled me closer. He gently pushed my chin up with his thumb, his lips brushing against mine, before gently kissing my temple. Something in this gesture, tender and so different from our raw lust and hunger, made me feel like I could melt into the sunny afternoon.

"Alright, I will see you later? Dinner?" I suggested.

"Sounds great."

I waved back at him and, gripping my notebook, I ventured deeper into the garden.

The roses bloomed proudly in their designated corner, a riotous sea of red, pink, and white. Their delicate perfume filled the air, competing with the heady scent of honeysuckles cascading over the wooden arbour. A variety of butterflies flitted amongst the blossoms, adding to the charm.

The Jacobean garden was resplendent with an array of lilies and lavender, their vibrant hues peeking out between the meticulously pruned boxwood hedges. I allowed my fingertips to gently brush the velvety petals, the faint murmur of bees providing a soothing soundtrack to my evening stroll.

I wandered towards the herb garden next, my senses immediately assaulted by the intoxicating scent of thyme, basil, and rosemary. Neat rows of earthy-toned pots housed everything from peppermint to sage, their fragrant contents promising a bounty for the upcoming party.

The sun was now a mere whisper in the sky, the garden illuminated by the soft glow of the fairy lights we'd strung around. The sight was ethereal, the crickets adding their evening symphony to the tranquil tableau. A soft sigh escaped me, a mix of relief, pride, and an indescribable sense of joy.

Looking around at the lush greenery, the blooming flowers, and the twinkling lights, I felt a surge of accomplishment. We had breathed life back into the manor's garden, transforming it from a forgotten patch of land into a vibrant Eden. I couldn't help but marvel at the transformation - it was a tangible representation of our sweat, determination, and stubborn refusal to give in.

I also liked how in the process the garden party was no longer just about Thornvale Manor; it was about celebrating a community. And unexpected connections, I added, looking at Heath kneeling in the distance, getting rid of some final stubborn weed.

I smiled.

The Thornvale Tamer, indeed.

Chapter 25

We'd been working side by side, an array of flowers surrounding us, their sweet fragrance mingling with the scent of the damp earth. The earlier tension, sparked by one of his playful comments, had been simmering between us, only amplified by the closeness.

His stormy blue eyes held mine, radiating a warmth that curled low in my belly. His shirt was discarded, his skin gleaming with sweat as he worked.

The sight sent a jolt of anticipation through me, my own lips parting involuntarily.

"You're good with your hands, Jasmine," Heath commented, his gaze lingering on me with an intensity that made my heart skip a beat.

I looked at him, an eyebrow raised in amusement, "Why, Heath, are you implying something?"

His laughter echoed through the garden, his eyes dancing with mirth. "I'm just admiring your gardening skills. But if you have something else in mind, who am I to stop the flow of creativity?"

His teasing reply was a flirtatious dance around the obvious tension, a dance we had become quite accustomed to. It stirred a thrill within me, and I responded with a grin, "Don't get carried away, Heath. We're here to work."

"Well, working with you is a pleasure, Jasmine," he replied, his voice dipping lower.

"Is it now?" I teased, returning his flirtatious banter with equal enthusiasm. The sexual tension between us was a simmering pot threatening to boil over, making even the simplest of conversations a challenge. That was one thing that I didn't expect: how hard it would be to work alongside him.

"Well, you know," he began, a cocky grin tugging at the corner of his lips, "you in that short dress amidst the flowers...it's a sight that could make even the best gardener forget his manners."

His words, laced with a distinct flirtatious undertone, sent a tingle down my spine. Heat bloomed in my cheeks. The morning sun seemed to match, matching the tension radiating between us.

"Oh really?" I shot back, raising a brow, trying to maintain my composure under his intense gaze.

The teasing grin didn't leave his face, instead growing wider. He stepped closer, the air between us thick with anticipation. I could smell the faint scent of his cologne, a strange and almost desolate note of charcoal and leather that perfectly suited his confident demeanour.

"Oh, definitely," he whispered, his voice dropping an octave, causing a shiver to run down my spine. "In fact, if you keep showing up like this, I might forget we're here to garden at all."

The loud ping drew our attention in the instant. Heath plucked his phone from his trousers and opened the emails. A frown of deep consternation etched on his usually calm face.

"It's Bradshaw," he muttered, the name coming out like a curse. "He's pushing to finalise the sale."

I leaned over to peek at the offending email, the curtly worded text confirming Heath's statement. The ruthless hotel developer was indeed eager to sink his claws into Thornvale Manor. My heart clenched at the thought, but I pushed away the panic, reminding myself that we had a plan.

"Can you keep him off our backs for a little bit longer?" I asked, trying to keep my voice steady. "We've come too far now. We can't let Bradshaw turn Thornvale into one of his soulless hotel monstrosities."

Heath looked at me, the weight of Thornvale Manor's future clearly pressing down on him. "It's all about the finances… I love the idea of the party, but I just don't know how much income it would realistically generate. And if it does… who knows if it continues to do so?"

I shrugged, trying to project an aura of confidence. "There's only one way to find out, right? Worst case scenario, we'll have one heck of a party. "Heath rubbed his temples, the strain evident in his posture. I reached out and gently shut down his phone, cutting off the cold, business-like glare of the screen. "I know you are worried;

we all are. But let's get back to work. The garden is looking well; people are confirmed to attend, and we can investigate the finances afterwards. Step by step."

He nodded, returning to trimming the maze.

In those last few weeks, I have thrown myself into gardening and organising the party, getting more and more excited about it. But the reality was Heath was right. We couldn't be sure if the party would work, or if it did once, whether the wider plan of opening the gardens to the public and perhaps hosting weddings or birthdays would ever even work. We had to try, yes, but the worry was still there, prickly like a thorn.

The afternoon went by, Heath getting busy getting the maze into shape. Meanwhile, I knelt by the rose bushes, wearing a sundress that was rapidly becoming more dirt than fabric. Too overwhelmed by my thoughts and trying to keep my focus on not chopping off my fingers with the shears, I didn't notice the sky turning grey.

Then, a distant rumble of thunder sounded. Within moments, the first drops of rain began to fall. Heath looked up, squinting into the sudden darkness. He got off his ladder and caught my eyes.

"It's looking a bit stormy!" he called out, getting the ladder and hurrying to put it back in the tool shed. I followed his lead, putting my gardening tools safely away. We closed the shed and checked whether there was anything else that we left that would not appreciate the rain.

"I haven't even checked the weather today, have you?"

Before I could reply, the sky opened, releasing a torrent of rain upon us. It was so sudden and violent that I couldn't help but find this situation amusing.

"Shit!" Heath yelled. "I forgot about the lawn mower next to the dahlias!"

"Let's get it back to the shed quickly!" I urged, running after him. "Looks like we're about to get soaked!" Startled laughter bubbled up from me as we were quickly drenched, the dirt on our clothes turning into mud. The rain was relentless. Heath grabbed the lawn mower, and I rushed to open the shed, making sure there was a space. Finally, it was safe from the raging skies.

"Let's go!" Heath yelled over the roar of the rain, his hand reaching out to me.

"The cottage is closer!" I shouted back, reaching his side. Our fingers intertwined, the familiar jolt of electricity shooting through me.

We made it to my cottage, drenched and breathless. Heath's clothes clung to him, highlighting the contours of his body. My dress was soaked, clinging to my skin. As I fumbled with the key to my front door, I couldn't help but steal glances at Heath, his chest heaving from the run, rain droplets clinging to his eyelashes.

We stumbled into the cottage, panting and dripping, laughter bubbling up from within us. Heath closed the door behind us with a click, which did little to shut down the sound of the roaring storm.

In the dim light, I could see the rainwater dripping from his dark hair.

"We need to get changed, and quickly. Don't want to get ill before the party," I pointed out.

"Yeah. As soon as it stops raining, I am going to run back to the manor."

"Should I make some tea in the meantime?

"Yes, please... Wait. Shit," Heath's eyes widened, a sudden realisation crossing his mind. "I don't have the key to the manor. I left it inside."

"Surely Mrs Butterworth will let you in?"

"She won't," he pressed his lips together. "Because she isn't there. She requested an emergency leave: her sister's birthday was meant to be in a couple of days, but she moved it this evening because of some good deal of last-minute holidays. But I forgot to take my key from the house because I forgot she would be leaving."

"And, of course, Parker has a spare key, but he is also off."

"Y-ees." Heath drawled.

"Wait, are you telling me... that you can't get back to the manor."

"Not until early afternoon tomorrow."

We stared at each other.

"So what you're telling me is that I am stuck with you till tomorrow?"

"Looks like it."

I let out a groan but smiled at him at the same time, letting him know I didn't mind. I put the kettle on and grabbed two mugs before moving towards the living room.

"Here," I said, handing him a plush blanket from the sofa. "You'll catch a cold."

Heath looked down at himself, his soaked shirt clinging to his well-defined muscles, the cold rain making him shiver. His gaze then shifted to me, a glint of mischief gleaming in his eyes.

"But, Jasmine, I have no spare clothes," he teased.

For a moment, my mind went blank, images flooding my thoughts. But I forced a laugh, crossing my arms over my chest. "Well, Heath, I don't think I have anything that would fit you."

"Not surprising, really."

After a moment, I found my voice. "You could… take them off," I suggested, my voice barely a whisper. I motioned towards another cosy blanket strewn over the back of my sofa. "You could ust sit under the blankets."

Heath's eyes darkened, and he stepped closer. The suggestive grin on his face was replaced with a more intense look, one that made my throat dry, and the spot between my legs wet. "Are you suggesting I get naked in your living room, Jasmine?"

"Yes. No! I mean, yes, because I don't want you to get ill."

I exhaled slowly.

His smirk widened, his midnight blue eyes twinkling in the candlelight. "Sure, sure."

Before I could reply, Heath began unbuttoning his shirt, his fingers deftly working at the buttons.

Soon, he was bare-chested, his shirt discarded on the floor. Despite the chill from his drenched clothes, his skin glowed in the warmth of the firelight. He wrapped the blanket around his waist, the fabric highlighting the V-line of his hips, his muscular chest on full display.

I turned on my heel, marching in my still-wet dress to the fireplace. I cradled a handful of kindling, adding some of the bigger logs. I struck a match.

The flame sputters to life, a tiny beacon in the growing twilight. It casts long, quivering shadows against the walls, painting the room in a warm glow. I hold it to the kindling, watching as the flame begins to consume the paper, then the wood.

The room was filled with the scent of rain and now, the comforting scent of the burning wood.

I glanced at Heath, who by now looked comfortable on the sofa, a blanket over most of his body. Still, my eyes linger for far too long on his bare shoulders.

"I am going to get changed," I announced quickly and ran upstairs, leaving a trail of water behind me.

Inside the bedroom, I could finally take a deep breath.

Outside, the storm raged on, sheets of rain battering against the windows with relentless force. My dress clung to my skin, a cold, uncomfortable second layer.

I peeled off my soaked dress, shivering as the cool air hit my damp skin. I caught a glimpse of myself in the mirror. With my tousled hair and flushed cheeks, I looked like a wayward mermaid who accidentally stumbled into the suburbs.

As the dress hit the floor with a wet splat, I reached for the towel hanging on the back of the door. A warm, dry outfit is the next logical step, but instead, my gaze wandered towards my underwear drawer. I opened it, and there, at the back, hidden behind the practical everyday cotton, was the lacy lingerie set I'd bought on a whim.

I lifted the bra and the thong, holding them up to the light. They are in the softest shade of pink, delicate, and impossibly tiny. They would probably create an itchy nightmare around my waist, and yet, they scream seduction. Heath was sitting downstairs, and I could feel his presence deep inside my bones. Would he notice?

Would I want him to notice?

Before I had a chance to change my mind, I slipped into the lingerie.

If this night was going to be unpredictable, I thought I might as well match the mood. The lace was surprisingly comfortable, clinging in all the right places. The colour was a soft blush against my skin.

With a satisfied smile, I reached for the oversized grey jumper and a pair of shorts, the answer to my previous question loud and clear in my head.

Yes. I wanted Heath to see what I was wearing underneath all the practical clothes.

Downstairs, my unexpected guest was checking his phone.

"The signal is out."

"Oh great. If a stray serial killer was to find us, that would be it."

"I sincerely hope that weather would dissuade even a serial killer from venturing outside."

"I hope so," I checked that the tea was properly brewed and brought the mugs back to the sofa, making myself comfortable next to Heath.

He started talking about something, but I could barely focus, the realisation that he was so close and completely naked, the lace of my lingerie burning my skin. My eyes were drawn to his bare chest, the muscles catching the flickering firelight, the dusting of hair leading down to the mystery hidden beneath the blanket. His arm was casually thrown over the back of the sofa, displaying a casual kind of confidence that only deepened my affection for him.

With Heath so close, I could barely focus on the conversation.

He turned towards me, a smile playing on his lips. "What are you thinking about, Jasmine?" he asked.

"That I should have checked the weather forecast," I rolled my eyes in mock annoyance. As if in response to that, the thunder boomed.

The cottage was still, except for the occasional flash of lightning and rumbling thunder outside. Rain pelted against the windows as Heath told tales of Thornvale Manor's history. I found myself captivated not only by the stories but also by him - the low rumble of his voice, the warmth of his body next to mine, and the way his eyes lit up as he spoke.

Suddenly, the lights flickered and then, with a sudden plunge, everything went dark. I jumped, and Heath's hand instinctively found mine, his grip firm and comforting. The storm had taken out the power.

"Oh, great," I groaned. "Wait here," I instructed, getting up to fumble my way to the kitchen for some candles.

By the dim light that trickled in through the rain-streaked windows, I found a box of half-used candles and a box of matches. The scent of old wax filled my nostrils as I brought them back to the living room, my heart pounding. Heath was a dark silhouette against the pale light from the windows, and my breath hitched as he rose to meet me.

"Let me help," he said, his voice smooth in the hushed darkness. His fingers brushed against mine as he took a few candles and matches. The contact sent sparks shooting up my arm, hotter than any flame.

We moved together, Heath lighting up the candles, and me, placing them around us in the room.

Once we were done, we found ourselves standing close, the warm glow enveloping us. Heath's gaze was intense, his eyes darker in the candlelight. My breath hitched as he reached out, tucking a loose strand of hair behind my ear.

"Maybe we should tell ghost stories to complete the mood. What do you think?"

"Ghost stories? Really, Jasmine?" Heath mocked.

"Well, it's traditional. Stormy night, no power, middle of nowhere…" I trailed off, teasing him. "Have you not done it before?"

He groaned, and the conversation rolled into our memories of childhood bonfires, of ghost stories, and we laughed and talked, interrupted only by the continuous sound of the thunder.

Every so often, his fingers brushed against mine, a spark of contact that sent my heart racing.

"Heath, have you not just told me this story about Jasper?" I noticed he was as distracted as I was. For a moment, he said nothing, his eyes leaving mine only to lazily drop onto my lips.

"Jasmine," he murmured, breaking the comfortable silence. His voice was low, a husky note that sent a flutter through me.

"Yes?" I replied, my voice barely above a whisper.

His eyes met mine, their usual hue darker in the candlelight. There's a question in them, an unspoken request for permission.

He shifted, the blanket rustling softly. For a moment, I caught a glimpse of the sharp lines of his hips, the trail of dark hair, the teasing hint of more hidden beneath the fabric. My heart skipped a beat, a delicious thrill rushing through me. His hand reached towards me.

"Can I...?" He started, but I was already nodding.

I breathed. "I thought you'd never ask."

Chapter 26

He stood up, letting the blanket roll onto the floor. My eyes widened. The soft glow of the candlelight painted Heath in warm hues, casting deep shadows that highlighted the contours of his body: his rigid, defined muscles and the hardness of his erection. My mouth went dry, and slowly, I took off my jumper and shorts.

He hissed, his eyes lit up when I revealed the delicate lace hugging the curves of my body.

"Come here," he commanded, and I took a few steps forward. I started tracing it with my hand, and he let out a low, deep growl. He unclasped my bra, his eyes never leaving my breasts. I gasped as his fingers brushed against my nipples, hard from cold and desire. I pushed my thumbs behind my panties, stepping away from them, letting myself be completely bare. Heath's features turned ravenous, and his hands gripped my waist, holding me close. I felt his pulse racing and how much he tried to hold back.

"I could take you, hard and fast, until all you remember is my name," he whispered. "And God knows how much I want to do that… But not tonight," he cupped my face and broke the kiss for a moment.

"Not tonight," I repeated, my tongue heavy, my brain turning to mush.

"No," he murmured. "Tonight, I want to enjoy every part of you. I want to savour all of you, Jasmine."

I could barely stand the feeling of being pressed against him, my softness against his hardness. I tilted my head, letting him kiss me deeper. His hand travelled down, and I arched my back, urging his hand to go lower. His tongue circled the tip of my breast, his hand brushing against my thigh, the graze of his nails almost unbearable - I needed him to touch me harder.

When he slid his fingers inside me, I let out a moan of relief. But it wasn't enough; it still wasn't enough.

Gently, he eased me onto the sofa, prying my legs open. Naked and vulnerable against his gaze, I shivered, pleasure overwhelming me when his lips brushed against my thighs.

He looked up from between my legs, and the sight of him was enough to make me come.

But then his tongue touched my core, softly first, then pressing a bit harder onto my flesh, letting it run downward. He groaned against my wetness, and the sound reverberated in my veins, my blood pulsing, harder and faster, matching the strokes of his tongue. His hair brushed my belly, and his stubble scraped against my sensitive flesh, the sensation overwhelming. He slid one finger inside me, and I arched my back, desperate for more. Heath pressed his hand atop my abdomen, keeping me still.

With a finality, he flickered his tongue, and my toes curled. Release claimed, the pleasure so intense I cried out, the sound of my voice muffled by the roar of the thunder.

"Heath…" I shook my head, both satisfied and utterly shocked. His face was flushed as he gave me a tentative smile and lazily stood up. His eyes scanned my body with admiration.

I had no idea I could feel like this - that someone else could make me feel like this.

Nonchalantly, Heath wrapped a blanket around his waist, and I put on my panties and jumper, noticing for the first time the chill in the room. Silence fell upon us, and I wracked my brain for something to say: what does one say after climaxing into the lips of a man whom I never expected to hook up with?

"I'd sleep here," Heath pointed out at the sofa.

Disappointment washed over me.

"You can… I guess you can share a bed with me?" I suggested, cursing myself internally for sounding so hesitant.

Still, he cocked his head, interested.

"Are you sure?"

"Yes," I nodded. "At least we will be warm," I shrugged, feigning ignorance. Heath smiled wickedly but didn't reply, following me to the bedroom instead.

The small bedroom looked impossibly cosy, and Heath towered in the space.

"Erm… should we go to bed, then? Unless you have… other plans?"

Jasmine, that was just cringe. I shuddered inside.

His smirk grew wider. "A hot shower to start," he said, the look in his eyes playful. "But I could always be convinced to change my plans."

Laughing softly, I brushed past him, letting my hand graze his bare chest. "I'll consider it," I teased, lips curling into a coy grin. "But don't take too long. The storm might just lull me to sleep."

Heath captured my wrist gently, pulling me close. "Guess I'll have to make it quick then," he whispered huskily, his eyes lingering on mine for just a heartbeat too long.

I inhaled and swallowed hard, breaking eye contact. I pulled out a fresh towel and handed it to him.

"Just give me a few minutes, and you can shower," I mumbled, disappearing into the bathroom.

I splashed my face with cold water and brushed my teeth, trying to calm my trembling body down.

I had sex with Heath Thornvale.

And I have never felt so good.

Despite my legs still shaking, I took myself upstairs, letting Heath use the bathroom. I put on my pyjamas and listened to the soft murmur of the shower as I climbed into bed.

Howling winds pushed against the windows, and raindrops tapped persistently, a fierce tempo that made the walls seem thin. The scent of rain mingling with earth trailed through the slight crack in the window, and I exhaled.

I could hardly believe what just happened.

Climbing in beside me, his body was a solid wall of warmth on my side, making me hyper-aware of the sliver of space that separated us.

Breaking the silence, he asked, his voice husky, "Comfortable, Jasmine?"

"As much as one can be while sharing a bed," I retorted, trying to keep my voice steady, ignoring the butterflies in my stomach.

He chuckled, the sound deep and soothing.

"Also, not just any bed. My bed," I pointed out. "So don't get too comfortable."

"Technically, my bed, seeing as I legally own the cottage," he added, a hint of mischief in his voice.

"Your bed," I echoed, a small smile tugging at my lips. "Does that make you a bed sheriff?"

"If it does, are you ready to abide by my laws?"

"Depends on the laws," I quipped back, a teasing smile on my lips. His body shifted, and suddenly he was closer, the gap between us disappearing. I could feel his breath on my face, his eyes looking down into mine. "First law," he murmured, his voice dropping lower, "No clothes allowed."

His bold declaration sent a rush of warmth through me, my heart pounding against my chest.

Despite the playful tone, his words had a deeper implication that was impossible to ignore.

"I like this law." I slid out of my pyjamas.

He reached out, his hand brushing against my arm, sending a shiver down my spine. His touch was light, and I let out a frustrating groan. His eyes held mine, the teasing glint replaced with an intense desire that mirrored my own. "I wonder," he murmured, "just how much heat you can handle, Jasmine."

The implication behind his words, the promise of something more, made my heart hammer against my chest. The intensity of his gaze and the suggestive tone of his voice set my pulse racing.

But I wasn't about to back down. "Guess you'll have to stick around and find out, won't you?" I retorted, meeting his intense gaze with a daring one of my own.

His eyes twinkled with amusement and a touch of admiration. "I was hoping you'd say that," he said, his voice husky.

Turning to face him, I gathered my courage, meeting his dark eyes.

With a swift move, he was hovering over me, his body warm and inviting. His lips were just inches from mine. "Oh, Jasmine," he whispered.

And with that, he closed the remaining distance between us, his lips capturing mine in a heated kiss. My hand closed around his hardness, exploring the silky flesh as he moaned into my neck, trailing the kisses down to the peak of my breasts. His hand travelled down, between my legs, and he teased me before I groaned with a mock frustration.

"I want more of you," I opened my eyes, staring at him with boldness that surprised me. "I want *all* of you," I clarified.

"Can you take all of me?" he teased, cocking his eyebrow.

"I like a challenge," I chuckled softly. My hands gripped him, and he held his breath, the time suddenly slowing down.

I guided him inside me, gasping as he filled me. I wrapped my legs around him, and a low sound of need filled the space. For a moment, he didn't move, and I savoured the sensation of my body opening itself for him before he slowly started to move, his fingers digging into the bed. I gave myself over to him, and with each thrust, the release inside me was building.

I pushed my hips against him, driving him deeper inside me. He murmured my name into the name, the sound of it making my whole body tremble. The rain intensified, and so did our rhythm, the slowness replaced by the raw need.

This man would be the end of me.

"Jasmine," his voice cut through the sensations, "look at me."

I obeyed, my eyelashes fluttering as I opened my eyes.

And then, as the storm raged, we climaxed, hands pressed together, eyes locked on each other. The rain lashed against the small cottage as I felt him pulsing inside me, his own pleasure mixing with mine.

"This was…" he breathed out, shaking his head. "My God, you are gorgeous, Jasmine."

I smiled.

We stayed wrapped around in each other's arms, silent and content, for a while. Later, Heath placed a kiss on top of my head and, murmuring about having a good night's sleep, he closed his eyes. Within minutes, his breath stilled, peaceful and heavy.

Soon enough, I fell asleep, too, his heavy hand on my waist. And as sleep claimed me, I silently hoped that the storm would last forever so we never had to leave the cottage.

Chapter 27

But of course, we had to.

I stirred from my sleep, a soft sigh escaping my lips as the dreamy haze of slumber dissipated. My body felt warm and deliciously tangled with Heath's, a gentle reminder of the night we'd shared.

Heath Thornvale.

I turned to look at him, his face peaceful in sleep, the soft light playing over the planes and angles of his handsome features. His chest rose and fell gently, his warmth a comforting presence against my side.

The memories of last night flooded in, and a warmth spread through me. The scent of him, his touch - everything was etched vividly in my mind.

"Morning," Heath's voice rumbled from behind me, his eyes still closed, the corners of his lips tugging upwards in a lazy smile.

I chuckled, wriggling out from his embrace and sitting up. "It's afternoon, Sleeping Beauty," I corrected him, my voice playfully teasing.

His eyes fluttered open at that, his gaze meeting mine. A flash of surprise passed through his eyes before he chuckled, running a hand through his dishevelled hair. "Is it?"

I nodded, a smirk playing on my lips. "Yes, it is. Seems like we were so exhausted after last night, we slept through the entire morning."

"I can't help it if someone kept me up all night."

My face turned a bright shade of red, his teasing words sending my heart into overdrive. "Oh, so it was my fault?" I countered, fighting to keep my voice steady.

His laughter filled the room, the sound making my heart flutter. "Yes, Jasmine, it was all your fault. Yours, and that beautiful body of yours." He paused, searching my face. "Do you… regret it?" he asked, a hint of seriousness creeping into his voice.

I pretended to ponder over his question, my lips twitching with suppressed laughter. "Well," I began, my tone deliberately contemplative. "I regret not having kicked you out of bed for stealing all the covers."

"Silent Cover Thief: duly noted." He leant over to kiss me. We stayed like this for a while, enjoying ourselves, before we finally pulled apart.

"Hey," I nudged him gently, watching as his eyelashes fluttered open to reveal those soulful blue eyes. "You want some coffee?"

Heath blinked at me, looking slightly bewildered, before breaking into a lazy grin. "You're offering to make coffee?" he asked, a teasing glint in his eyes. "You must really like me."

I snorted, swatting his chest playfully. "Don't flatter yourself, Thornvale. I'm just ensuring you're sufficiently caffeinated before I put you to work in the garden."

Heath chuckled, his laughter warm and rich, filling the room and making my heart skip a beat. "Fair enough," he said, pulling me in for a quick kiss. "I can't wait."

Padding softly to the kitchen, the smile lingered on my face. I glanced at the weather outside, still gloomy and grey, as if sulking after being subjected to the violence of the storm...

The storm.

As if led by some strange gut instinct, I flung open the cottage door.

My heart plummeted as I took in the sight before me. Our once flourishing garden lay in ruins. Flowers uprooted, trees battered, their once lush leaves strewn across the lawn like discarded confetti. A mournful sigh escaped me as I took a tentative step forward, the devastation swallowing me whole. It was like a punch to the gut.

I could see the rose bushes that Heath had painstakingly pruned, now stripped of their vibrant blooms, looking desolate and beaten. The trellis, where climbing vines had begun to crawl and weave their magic, lay on its side, the vines a mangled mess.

Tears stung at my eyes as I walked further into the heart of the destruction. We had invested so much of our time and effort, pouring our heart and soul into restoring the garden. It felt like we had lost more than just plants and flowers.

But we gained something too, a niggling voice in my mind reminded me. Only that whatever happened last wouldn't save the garden from the claws of the ruthless hotel developer.

My shoulders sagged, and a lump formed in my throat. We had been preparing for the garden party for weeks, and now, all our efforts seemed in vain.

I felt a hand on my shoulder and turned to find Heath standing beside me. His eyes mirrored my sadness as he took in the scene of devastation.

"It's bad, isn't it?" I muttered, trying to keep my voice steady, but the despair seeping into my tone was unmistakable. Heath's heavy hands rested on my shoulders and started to rub them gently.

"Let's go and have a proper look around," he finally suggested. "We need to know the extent of the damage."

I nodded. If I tried to speak, there would be no sound but a sob. I knew Heath was right; I knew we had to assess the damage quickly, but I was scared to face it. I wanted to go back to last night, when the sound of rain and thunder was soothing, when all I could feel was Heath's touch and the safety of the cottage.

Don't be pathetic, Jasmine.

We agreed to meet in an hour in the garden, Heath disappearing to get a shower and find fresh clothes. Walking into the garden was like walking into a graveyard. I swallowed hard.

"Looks like the storm really had its way," he murmured, his voice low and thoughtful. His eyes swept across the disarray, taking in the uprooted flowers, the broken branches, and the bench that had been knocked over on its side. The lush green carpet of the lawn was littered with branches, some torn away by the vicious winds, others violently snapped in two.

"I can't believe this," I swallowed har, my voice tight as I ran my hand through my tousled hair.

Silence descended upon us, the severity of the destruction a weight that pushed away any room for words. Our footsteps echoed through the chaos as we began to navigate what was left of the garden. I took mental notes on what needed to be fixed but gave up halfway. There was simply so much to do.

"I am going to go back and… look over those details of the contract that Bradshaw sent," Heath finally said, his voice devoid of any emotions.

"Heath, no," I protested. "We can think of something…"

"Of what? Jasmine, people won't come and see *this*. And we were meant to send some photos of the garden to the web designer - not much to send now." He added bitterly.

"But-"

"I am sorry, Jasmine. We tried, we really did. I honestly appreciate your help; you have no idea how much. But I am just being realistic," he looked at me sadly. "I will see you later, at dinner?"

I pressed my lips together as I watched him walk away.

Still, I didn't want to give up. I couldn't.

Branch by branch, I began to clear the debris, my hands protected by thick gloves as I tossed the fallen limbs into a growing pile.

As the morning went on, fatigue set in. My muscles ached, and my back protested with every bend, but it was the emotional toll that was hitting me hardest. This garden, these flowers, they weren't just plants and trees.

An undercurrent of anger bubbled up inside me, a hot, desperate frustration at the unfairness of it all. We didn't deserve this. Our garden didn't deserve this.

A particularly stubborn branch snapped under my rough handling, the jarring sensation reverberating up my arms. I stood there for a moment, panting, a broken branch in my hands.

And then the tears came, unbidden and relentless. *I'm angry, I'm upset, I'm exhausted!* I screamed in my head, breathing heavily, staring at the destroyed garden.

I reached out for my phone and took some photos, sending them to Caro. She responded by asking if we could talk, and I said I would call her in half an hour.

But then I noticed something else, an email notification on my phone. I opened it, and my eyes widened.

The job offer from the famous London landscaping company.

I stared at the email. The words on the screen danced in front of my eyes.

Perhaps this is it, I thought. My sign that I should just leave Thornvale Manor and get back to my London life. The universe, quite frankly, couldn't be louder.

I pushed my phone back into the pocket of my jeans and marched back to the cottage, swallowing the remnants of the tears. I should be realistic about it: I was simply employed as a gardener. I did my job, and it wasn't my fault that the storm destroyed everything. I got offered a job that I wanted. It was all *good*.

Then why didn't it feel like that?

I called Caro.

"What's happened?" she asked, concerned.

"It's ruined," I blurted out, the words tumbling from my lips. "We had a storm last night. The garden's in shambles."

There was a moment of silence before Caro responded. "Oh, shit, Jasmine. I'm so sorry. I know how much this meant to you. This is really, really shit."

"Understatement of the year." I sighed. "And I got this London job I told you about."

"That's… good. Right? You really wanted it."

"It is, yes. But things got a bit complicated since I applied."

"Look, Jasmine, I know you're upset about the garden. It makes sense. But you don't need to make any decisions right now. Just sit on it."

I sighed, a wave of gratitude washing over me. Caro always knew how to handle my crises. But I had yet to drop the second, considerably more explosive, bombshell.

"It's not just the garden. There's more," I admitted, biting my lip. "And it's about Heath."

"You two finally figured out how to have a conversation without glaring at each other?"

I laughed, the nervous tension easing a bit. "We've...progressed a bit beyond that, Caro. We slept together."

"What!" Caro exclaimed. "But how did that happen? Last time I checked, you two couldn't stand each other!" She tapped her bottom lip. "But then again, there is a fine line between love and hate."

"And let's just say we jumped that line." I agreed. "Wait, no, what love?" I frowned at her. "It was just… lust."

"Just lust! You don't even believe it yourself," Caro pointed out.

"I just don't know what to think. Everything was going so well, and now… Heath is back to wanting to sell the manor. Garden is destroyed. I got a job in London. And my employment ends in two weeks, so I guess 'just lust' is probably the easiest to digest."

"I hear you. But you are still at Thornvale Manor for two weeks. Let's see what happens."

"Yeah," I exhaled.

"Was the sex good?"

"It was just… ," I grinned at her and let out a long, suggestive exhale.

"Well, there you go, then. At least sex was great. Could have been worse."

"I can always count on you to put things into perspective," I said, laughing despite myself. "What would I do without you?"

"I dread to think," she replied, her voice full of warmth. "I dread to think."

The only problem was that as soon as we hung up, I was left alone.

So, with trembling hands, I dialled my mother's number, my eyes never leaving the devastated garden. The phone rang twice before she picked up. I invited her to come visit me in the cottage for dinner, and I texted Heath that I won't be joining him tonight.

I needed people around me, and my parents have always been very supportive. Dad was already attending his best friend's birthday party, and I made Mum swear that she would make sure he got there. There was no need, I told her, for Dad to do a U-turn and leave his best mate hanging.

Which was how, as soon as twilight descended on the Thornvale estate, my Mum was standing in the doorway.

"Hello, dear," her warm voice greeted me. It was a comfort, something familiar and soothing amidst the chaos.

"Mum," I choked out. "The garden... it's ruined."

I heard her sharp intake of breath, and I knew she understood the depth of my distress.

"Oh, Jasmine," she sighed. "I'm so sorry, dear."

Tears welled up in my eyes, threatening to spill over. "The storm was... it was horrible, Mum. All the plants, the trees... we worked so hard on them."

"I know, sweetheart," Mum replied gently. "But remember, nature has its own way of healing. The garden will come back to life, just give it time. It's just a setback."

I bit my lip, trying to stave off the tears. "But the garden party, Mum... we'd invited the entire community. They were supposed to see the garden at its best."

There was silence for a moment before Mum spoke again. "Jasmine," she said, her voice steady and full of conviction. "The people in our community are not coming to the party to judge your gardening skills. They are coming to support you. Whether the garden is in full bloom or not, they will be there."

Despite my heavy heart, a small smile tugged at the corners of my lips. Mum had always had a way of making things seem better. "You like, really think so?"

"Of course," Mum reassured me. "Jasmine, you're not the only one affected by it. The storm... it did a number on the entire town. Mr. Heatherwick's greenhouse, remember? It's gone. The community centre lost its roof, and half the town is without power. It had honestly been a hell of a storm, and everyone will understand. Do you think the party can still go ahead?"

"I don't know. We have less than a week to at least clear the garden - there is no way it would look like before. I just worry we won't have time to even finish the cleaning before Sunday."

"Why don't Dad and I help?" She suggested.

"Thanks, Mum, but no, honestly…"

"Seriously! It would be fun! And I get to meet the mysterious lord of the manor," she winked. Blush crept up my neck. I should probably tell her about me and Heath, but I had zero energy for my Mum's puppy-like excitement and energy right now.

"At least think about it," she said firmly, and I sighed. Once Arlene Ackerley decided something, it was happening. "Let's have some food, okay? I brought some lasagne."

"I said I'd cook," I reminded her.

"Jasmine, dear, would you really want to cook now?"

"Not really," I admitted. "But how did you know?"

"I am your mother," she said with a finality that explained everything. She unpacked the lasagne and put it in the oven, busying herself with preparing the table whilst I got out the chilled wine.

"I was so impressed by this building. It's been years since I've visited Thornvale Manor," Mum was saying. "Stunning grounds, honestly, if not too vast for my liking. And there was this charming butler who pointed me in the direction of the cottage-"

"*Charming* butler?" I nearly choked on my words.

"Oh, yes," she nodded enthusiastically. "Parker, I think, his name is?"

I stared at her in disbelief.

"I need a drink," was all I managed to say.

Chapter 28

I woke up to another gloomy, grey day as if the world couldn't shake off the horrible storm. I rubbed my eyes and pushed myself to sit up, my back against the raised pillow.

Outside, I could see the poor, mauled garden.

But even amidst the destruction, there were signs of resilience. A few flowers still clung to their stems, their colours a stark contrast against the dreary backdrop. Tiny buds were still intact on some branches, promising a future bloom.

The garden party is going to happen, I thought.

Yes, the scene outside may be more "Survivor: English Garden" than "Jane Austen's Tea Party". But the more I pondered the idea, the more it made sense, especially given what Mum said. There was still time to clean the garden, so at least it wasn't a hazard for the guests, and I had a plan in mind. Parker's welcome home party actually inspired it - we were going to basically decorate the hell out of this garden. And, I thought, as I marched to the bathroom to wash my face, there would be lots of food and drinks and people, and there was still a very good chance that although we couldn't showcase the garden, we could give people a good time.

I texted Heath:

Emergency meeting in the drawing room - ask Mrs B and Parker to join, please?

He responded immediately with a thumbs-up emoji.

An hour later, I headed to the drawing room. It was shrouded in an unspoken dread as I walked in, their faces shadowed by the pallor of disappointment.

"Hi everyone," I said.

"Tea?" Mrs Butterworth suggested, and I nodded. "There is no way we are handling a crisis without a good, proper Earl Grey," she concluded.

"Wise words. Okay, so we all saw what happened," I started, gesturing with a casual wave towards the window that looked out onto the garden, its beauty now marred by upturned plants and broken branches. "Our plans took a nosedive, quite literally, but hear me out. The party will still happen. We're just going to have to be... creative."

Parker grumbled something that I chose to ignore. Heath simply watched me, uncertainty glinting in his eyes.

"Pardon me, Jasmine," Mrs. Butterworth began, her forehead creasing. "But the garden...it's been pretty much *ravaged* by the storm. I looked this morning, and it just… it's nothing like what it was before."

"I know," I replied, trying to keep my voice steady. "But the people of Sagebourne didn't sign up to see a perfect garden. They signed up to see Thornvale

Manor come alive again. And that's exactly what we're going to give them."

Heath's eyebrows were now raised. Parker grumbled, his arms crossed, looking about as cheerful as a storm cloud. "And how, pray tell, do you suggest we do that?"

"Enchantment, Parker," I said, allowing a smile to creep onto my face. "We may not have flowers, but we have lights, balloons and other decorations. We're going to fill the garden with lanterns and fairy lights. Every path, every corner, it's going to glow. And decorations, we can hang them from the trees, the arbours, the railings. If we can't bring them to a garden party, we'll bring them to a fairyland."

Heath finally spoke. His voice was thoughtful. "It's going to be a lot of work. Not just the decorations but clearing up the garden."

"It will," I agreed, nodding. "But it's work we can do together."

For a moment, silence hung in the room. Then Mrs. Butterworth nodded, her face determined. "We'll make it happen," she said with firm confidence. "I agree with what Jasmine is saying. We can make it happen."

"My parents found a good gardening company, and they called them today: they said they'd be able to send three gardeners to help with clearing up as soon as tomorrow morning," I told them. This was after I told my Mum that there was no way Dad was doing it with his bad knee. But they still wanted to help, and when they told me this morning about the gardening company, I was overjoyed.

"Meanwhile, we can focus on getting the decorations, setting up some food stalls for the people, making sure we have everything ready. We have five days left. It's doable."

Silently, we all looked at Heath. It was his call, after all.

"Let's do it," he finally said. "Jasmine, please send me the details of the gardening company. Mrs B, are you still okay with the rose-themed food? There are a few rose blooms still left, so I think we can pull it off. I will confirm the catering company today as well. Jasmine, we can make a trip to town and get all the decorations."

A sense of relief washed over me. If Heath was on board, we could pull this off. #

As I finished speaking, the tension in the room was broken by an all too familiar sound.

I heard a soft 'meow' from the entrance of the room and looked down to see Buttons, the king of stealth, standing at the doorway. His sapphire eyes glinted with mischief as his gaze darted between Parker and me.

"Oh, no," I said, my voice laced with amusement. "The interloper arrives."

Parker's eyes narrowed as he spotted the feline intruder. "I swear, if that infernal creature does not remove itself…" He left the sentence hanging, his disdain palpable.

Parker's face contorted into a grimace that would rival a gargoyle's as he turned to face the cat. Buttons, as if sensing Parker's disapproval, halted in his tracks, one paw suspended in mid-air, and locked eyes with the butler.

"And what," Parker's voice was icy, his words as sharp as frost-tipped daggers, "do you think you're doing, you felonious feline?"

Buttons, however, seemed to thrive on Parker's hostility. He sauntered into the room with the audacious confidence of a royal prince. He meowed again, his tail high in the air, brushing past Parker's legs. Parker recoiled as if he'd been stung, his lips curled in a grimace.

"If you dare shed a single hair on this oriental rug, you...you fiend, I will personally make you into a pair of gloves," Parker threatened, shaking his fist at the entirely unimpressed feline. Buttons only blinked lazily, clearly unintimidated by the threat.

I couldn't help but chuckle at the scene. "Parker, are you sure you weren't a dog in a past life?" I asked, grinning at his unamused glare. "I mean, you and Buttons literally fight like cats and dogs."

Heath joined in the laughter while Mrs. Butterworth simply shook her head with a smile. "The day Parker and Buttons become friends," she murmured, "is the day the manor truly will have seen it all."

* * *

The afternoon sun cast a faint glow over the battered landscape as Heath and I piled into his vintage Aston Martin. Finally, the weather started to turn.

"I checked the weather for Sunday; it's looking like we will be having some sunshine," I told him. Heath nodded.

"That's good news."

"Also, I love the car," I added, genuinely impressed.

"It belonged to my grandfather," Heath explained. "It's definitely my favourite car."

We settled into a comfortable silence,

I glanced at Heath, his hands steady on the wheel, his eyes focused on the road ahead. He looked every bit the lord of the manor, right down to the slight frown of concentration that creased his brow. It was a look I found both endearing and, I admit, a bit sexy.

Okay, *very* sexy.

"You know," he began, "when you said we should still hold the party, I thought you were mad."

I feigned shock, placing a hand over my heart. "Mad? Me? Never."

A small smile tugged at the corners of his mouth. "But, having thought about it... I think it's a brilliant idea."

I blinked at him, surprised. "Really? You do?"

He nodded, his gaze never leaving the road. "Really. It's unconventional, sure. But it's also brave. And hopeful. It's... very you."

"Thank you," I smiled.

For the next few days, I helped the gardeners who joined us to clear the garden. Parker managed to fix a few pergolas and arbours, Mrs Butterworth simply lived in the kitchen, and Heath liaised with the locals, trying to make sure we had enough food and drinks.

And then, on Saturday, a day before the party, we were ready to decorate.

Chapter 29

As the sun began to set, Heath and I were in the garden, doing our best to transform the storm-stricken area into a place of celebration. The faint glow of the twilight bathed everything in soft, mellow hues, lending a touch of magic.

"Hand me that lantern, will you?" I asked, trying to reach a high branch of an apple tree.

Heath stepped closer, the lantern swinging from his hand. The warm glow illuminated his strong features, casting intriguing shadows on his face.

"Why don't I hang it?" he offered, his voice husky.

"It's fine," I argued, "I can reach–"

Before I could finish, Heath lifted me by the waist, effortlessly hoisting me up until I could easily hang the lantern. A surprised squeak escaped me, but the sudden proximity to Heath took my breath away.

"Problem solved," he said, his voice a low rumble that vibrated through me.

Heath gently lowered me back to the ground, but his hands lingered on my waist for a moment longer than necessary. My heart pounded in my chest at the contact, and I couldn't help but meet his gaze. There was a playful glint in his eyes that sent a flutter through my stomach.

"Well," he began, his voice low and teasing, "you could always keep needing help. I'd be more than willing to... assist."

His innuendo was clear, and I laughed, playfully pushing his chest. "Oh, you'd like that, wouldn't you?"

Heath's grin broadened as he nodded. "Very much."

We continued our work, hanging more lanterns, arranging chairs, but the undercurrent of tension never left us. Every brush of hands, each shared glance, amplified the palpable energy.

Working with Heath, preparing the garden for the party, felt surprisingly intimate. His casual touches sent shivers down my spine, and our continuous banter kept the atmosphere light and flirty.

As the last lantern lit up the garden, I took a step back, admiring our handiwork. The garden was still healing from the storm, but it held a charm of its own. It had weathered the storm, and so had we. There were still plenty of decorations to add, but even just the fairy lights and the lanterns already transformed the space.

"You know," Heath murmured, his voice pulling me from my thoughts, "the garden isn't the only thing that's benefitted from your touch."

His words hung in the air between us, a promise of something more, something deeper. And with a smile, I realised I was looking forward to exploring it.

As we set to work, the air was thick with a mix of determination and lingering desire. Heath and I moved through the garden, our bodies brushing against each other, sending electric currents through my veins.

Heath reached up, hanging lanterns from the branches of the trees, his movements confident and precise. His fingers lingered, the warmth of his touch seeping into my skin. I couldn't help but let out a teasing laugh.

"The lanterns are definitely looking good. You are doing a good job with them," I praised him.

"That's when I am not distracted." He turned to face me.

The tension between us thickened, the air crackling with anticipation. Every brush of his hand, every accidental touch, sent shivers down my spine, igniting a fire within me.

I stepped closer, my voice a mere breath away from his ear. "Is that so, Thornvale?" I whispered, my words dripping with mischief. "And what exactly would distract you?"

Heath's eyes darkened, his hands momentarily frozen. His lips brushed against the shell of my ear as he replied, his voice thick with desire, "You, Jasmine. You distract me in the most delicious ways."

My breath hitched, my heart racing as his words sent a surge of heat through me. I couldn't resist playing along, the playful banter between us electrifying.

"Well," I said, my voice dropping to a sultry tone, "if you can manage to stay focused, we might just get this garden ready in time."

Heath chuckled, his fingers resuming their task. "Challenge accepted," he murmured, his voice laced with determination. "But I make no promises. In fact," his fingers traced my waist, slowly stopping at the button of my shorts, "I am planning to lose that challenge right now."

The button popped open. He leant towards me, his tongue brushing my lips, before he flipped me around, my back now pressed against his hard chest. His hand travelled down my thongs, torturously slow, his fingers brushing my clit.

I moaned and arched my hips towards his hand. He pressed me harder so I could feel his erection against my lower back, which sent the sparks of desire low inside my belly. Finally, his fingers pressed against my clit, circling it slowly, and I moaned again, the friction almost unbearable.

When his fingers plunged deep inside me, I gasped softly. His other hand cupped my breasts, his thumb teasing my nipple. For a moment, I was happy to just leave the garden, to wrap my legs around him, to feel him inside me, hard and ready. For a moment, I wanted to let the garden be damned. I wanted Heath to pin me down to the soft grass beneath us, to let that sensation consume me. I gasped as he increased the pace until the wave of pleasure washed over me. My legs were shaking, and I struggled to keep myself standing.

Heath let me go softly, and I spun around.

"You've lost," I breathed heavily, somehow still thinking about the challenge.

"Have I now?" He smirked before he licked his fingers. "You're delicious," he said before picking up another lantern. "Back to work," he gave me a smug grin, and I groaned. My legs were still shaking as I continued decorating.

As the night wore on, the garden was transformed. There was still plenty to do in the morning, but even with the lanterns and fairy lights, the place looked completely different.

I put my head on Heath's shoulder, and his arm circled my waist. I listened to his relaxed, steady breathing as I admired the garden, bathed in the magical, soft shadows and lights. Tiny, twinkling points of light seemed to dance in the gentle wind. Then there were the lanterns hung from the branches of the few trees that had withstood the storm. They were paper spheres of soft pastels, casting an ethereal glow that painted the garden in shades of tranquillity. Their light was softer, more diffuse, filling the space with a sense of warmth and serenity.

It was beautiful.

Suddenly, the purr of the car's engine echoed in the distance.

"I think it might be Sienna and Jasper," Heath said, and we both headed towards the driveway.

Soon enough, Sienna and Jasper climbed out of Sienna's sports car - she messaged Heath earlier saying she would pick Jasper up from the airport, as his flight was delayed. She looked stunning in the white linen shirt and bermuda shorts.

"Hi, lovebirds," Sienna smirked.

Jasper looked at her, surprised, and then at me and Heath.

"I think I need a drink and an explanation," he grinned.

***

"So, it appears," Jasper began, his smirk devilish as he clinked his whiskey glass against mine, "that my dear older brother has been dipping his toe into more than just the gardening pool."

Heath choked on his beer mid-sip, and Sienna snorted into her gin and tonic. The patio lights twinkled above us, casting dancing shadows on the face of Thornvale Manor, making the scene feel more like a midsummer night's sitcom than a quiet family drink.

"Oh, please," I retorted, laughing and rolling my eyes, "the only pool your brother has been dipping his toes into is the pond when he missteps whilst weeding."

Sienna chortled and elbowed her brother.

Heath, having finally recovered from his near-death-by-beer experience, shot me an amused glance. "Believe it or not, Jasper, some of us are capable of developing relationships that aren't founded on late-night misadventures in Rome's nightclubs."

Jasper raised an eyebrow, still grinning. "My, my, Heath. Defending your honour? I haven't seen you this riled up since...well, never."

"And to think," Sienna added, "it took a storm-ravaged garden and Jasmine to bring it out."

Laughter rang around the table as Sienna shared another one of her outrageous travel stories, her eyes sparkling with mischief. She raised her wine glass for a toast, "To siblings! And to Jasmine, who somehow still hasn't run away!" I laughed as I clunk my glass against theirs.

At one point in the evening, when Jasper was in the middle of his story about his art gallery, I snuck out to the kitchen to bring more snacks.

"I am just here for the snacks," I smiled at Mrs Butterworth, who was leaning against the kitchen island, a mug of steaming tea in her hand. And then, in the dim light, I noticed her eyes glistened, watery and glazed.

Were there tears in her eyes?

"Mrs B," I placed my hand gently on her shoulder. "Are you alright?"

"Oh yes, child. Perfectly alright, in fact." I saw that she was gazing at the drawing room, which was seen from the kitchen, all three siblings laughing and joking. "I just haven't seen them like this since Lord Edward passed. I don't think all three of them were in the same room, let alone laughing and joking. It's as if not just the garden came alive." She paused. A small, singular tear traced a path on her cheek before falling. "I am glad Jasper offered you that gardening job, Jasmine." She squeezed my hand.

I squeezed back and smiled. "Me too."

Chapter 30

The day of the garden party had finally arrived.

I could barely sleep last night, tossing and turning. I woke up at the crack of dawn, rushing to the garden to finish off the decorating. Despite the early hours we were all busy, running in and out of the manor, trying to set everything up.

And finally, at four o'clock, just before the first guests arrived, everything was done.

I stood in the middle of the garden in a pastel blue dress, admiring the work.

The centrepieces were undoubtedly fairy lights, lots of them. Intertwined amongst the branches of the remaining trees, strung around the remnants of our pergolas, and wrapped around the roses, they lent a dreamy glow to the evening, casting dancing shadows that added to the mystical charm. A variety of antique, wrought iron and paper lanterns filled with candles, placed strategically throughout the garden, added an air of elegance and a soft, flickering light that complemented the fairy lights.

I also got yards of gauzy, white fabric. Draped between trees and from the gazebo, they swayed with the breeze, creating an ethereal ambience that echoed whimsical elegance. To add a touch of sophistication and elegance, I envisioned long, rustic wooden tables adorned with tall silver candelabras and vases filled with wildflowers, which were now standing proudly at the centre of the garden. The combination of natural elements with polished silverware made a beautiful contrast.

And, of course, no garden party would ever be completed without a comfortable seating area. Vintage garden furniture scattered with pastel-coloured cushions would invite our guests to relax and enjoy the surroundings. Lastly, I scattered oversized glass hurricane candle holders with white pillar candles all around the garden. They provided not only additional soft lighting, but their twinkling reflections would further enhance the magical aura.

The food stalls were heavy with local produce. On one of them, Mrs Butterworth's placed her own goods, specifically created to match our rose theme: rose macarons, rosewater panna cotta, rose and lemon cheesecake, and white chocolate and rose tart.

As the guests started to arrive, the transformed gardens of Thornvale Manor buzzed with life as laughter, and conversations filled the air. The sound of a local jazz band floated through the air, blending perfectly with the soft rustling of leaves in the summer breeze. Soon enough, the garden party was in full swing. The trees and plants were still in bad shape, but the rough edges left by the storm were softened by the elegant, whimsical decorations. I noticed my parents, who were proudly announcing to everyone that I was behind the restoration of the old garden.

Among the crowd, I spotted another familiar face – Jasper Thornvale.

His animated smile and easy charm were as welcoming as ever. He appeared genuinely delighted as he approached me, his eyes sparkling in the soft light of the lanterns and fairy lights.

"Jasmine, you've outdone yourself," he exclaimed, sweeping me up in an unexpected hug. "This is incredible!"

I laughed, feeling a blush creep up my cheeks at his praise. "Thank you, Jasper. I'm glad you like it."

"Like it? I love it!" He pulled back, his eyes roving over the blossoming flowerbeds, the manicured lawns, and the sparkling pond. "You've breathed life back into Thornvale Manor, Jasmine."

"Thank you, Jas. You know," I began, leaning in closer, "I've been thinking... I have plenty of ideas how to further help with the estate. For example, the garden would be the perfect place for a wedding."

Jasper choked on his sip of tea, his eyes widening in surprise. "A wedding?" he sputtered, a hint of panic in his voice. "You're not proposing, are you?"

I burst out laughing. "No, no, calm down, Mr. Commitment-Phobia. I was just thinking it would be a great location for someone else's wedding." I specified.

He gave me a mock glare, feigning offence. "Good. You nearly gave me a heart attack. You know I have a fear of being tied down."

I raised an eyebrow, unable to resist the opportunity for a little teasing. "Oh, I'm well aware, Jasper. But imagine the irony if you were the first one to get married there, after all those years of refusing to settle down."

He scoffed, but there was a glimmer of amusement in his eyes. "Ha! Not happening, Jasmine. I'll take being the eternal bachelor over a life sentence any day."

I leaned back in my chair, crossing my arms. "You know, one day, someone might just come along and change your mind. Just wait and see!"

He chuckled. "We'll see, Jas. We'll see. Anyway, as long as you're not plotting to lock me down, I'm all ears for this wedding talk."

I smirked, relishing the banter between us. "I wouldn't dream of locking you down, Jas. Just think about how stunning the garden would be with all the flowers, the fairy lights... it would be a dreamy setting for a couple's happily-ever-after."

He shook his head, a playful glint in his eyes. "I'll consider it, but only if you promise to be the one to handle all the wedding planning. I'm allergic to seating charts and bridesmaid dress fittings."

I laughed, enjoying the playful exchange. "Deal!"

We clinked our cups together, the sound of our laughter mingling with the ambient music. And who knew? Maybe, just maybe, one day, Thornvale Manor's garden would witness a wedding, even if it wasn't going to be Jasper's. Our conversation drifted then from the garden to his time in Rome and then, somewhat inevitably, to the topic of Heath. My heartbeat quickened at the mention of his name, a fluttery feeling taking root in my stomach.

"And how do you find Heath's company?" His question hung in the air between us, an expectant look on his face.

I hesitated, considering my words carefully. "Heath..." I was unsure where to start, "At first, I found him cold, almost unapproachable. But as I got to know him, I saw a different side of him. He's passionate about Thornvale, just like us."

Jasper nodded, a knowing smile gracing his lips. "And there's something else, isn't there?"

I bit my lip and nodded "Yes, there's something else."

Our conversation turned serious as he looked at me with a contemplative expression. "Jas, have you thought about staying? At Thornvale, I mean. The Manor could use a permanent gardener."

His proposition took me by surprise. I glanced back at the vibrant garden, my mind replaying the countless hours I had spent working on it. It felt like my sanctuary, a place that resonated with my love for nature. The thought of leaving it behind was unsettling - and yet still, there was that job offer in London. The HR was simply waiting for my answer, ready to onboard me as soon as I said yes.

"I've been thinking about it," I admitted. "This place... it feels like home."

Jasper nodded, his eyes soft. "And what about Heath? How does he fit into your plans?"

I bit my lip, a flurry of emotions flooding over me. Heath and I had grown close during our project, and our relationship had evolved in unexpected ways. He was no longer just Jasper's aloof brother; he had become someone special to me. Jasper was right: *how does his brother fit into my plans?*

"I... I'm not sure yet," I confessed, meeting Jasper's eyes. "But I'm willing to find out."

We were interrupted as Heath himself joined us, a playful smile on his face. "I hope I'm not interrupting something important."

Jasper laughed, patting his brother's shoulder. "Not at all, Heath. We were just discussing the future of Thornvale Manor. And Jasmine's part in it."

"Oh?"

"I think she should stay as a permanent gardener," Jasper announced happily. Heath's eyes widened in surprise, but before he could say anything, someone's voice rumbled next to us.

"Heath, old sport!" A middle-aged man with a pint of cider sauntered towards us. "I have been dying to catch up! I knew your old man, you see, and -,"

"Let's talk later," Heath mouthed, and I nodded with a smile.

As the evening wore on, filled with laughter, praise, and reminiscing, I couldn't help but feel a sense of home that I had spoken to Jasper before. I was here, amidst this beautiful garden with people I cared about, celebrating a victory that was so close to my heart.

A cheer from the crowd drew my attention to where Heath stood, raising a glass. He looked different from the cold, aloof man I had first met. The icy shield had melted away, replaced by a warm smile and relaxed demeanour.

He was in his element, charming the crowd with his easy conversation and undeniable charisma. He had a way of making everyone feel important, listening intently to their stories, nodding and laughing at the right moments. I found myself smiling at the sight, my heart fluttering.

Despite our rocky start and the challenges we faced, we had done it. Together, we brought the gardens back to life, and we were hopefully now on the way to preserve the heritage of Thornvale Manor and save it from the clutches of a ruthless hotel developer.

And then, amidst the hustle and bustle of the party, our eyes met. Heath raised his glass to me, a silent toast. A wave of gratitude surged within me. We had gone from reluctant partners to being each other's pillars of support. As I looked at Heath, I couldn't stop thinking that perhaps Thornvale Manor held more than just a summer job for me - perhaps it held my future, too.

Chapter 39

Underneath the diamond-studded night sky, the gardens of Thornvale Manor bathed in a warm, ethereal glow from the lanterns hanging from the trees. The garden party was a memory now, the last of the guests had departed hours ago, leaving behind a comforting silence. The scent of the jasmine flowers, heavy and sweet, wafted through the air, enhancing the charm of the night, though I realised with a sense of nostalgia that they would soon stop blooming.

Heath and I sat on the table outside the cottage, our bodies close but not quite touching, the rustling of the night breeze was the only sound breaking the silence. The peace of the moment was such a stark contrast to the whirlwind of emotions that had swept us up in recent weeks that I exhaled loudly with relief. We didn't know whether the garden party would bring visitors, but it was always worth a try.

"Heath," I started, breaking the comfortable silence. "About what Jasper said—"

He cut me off, turning to me with a seriousness in his eyes that made me pause. "Jasmine," he began, his voice barely above a whisper, "I have something I need to say."

A knot formed in my stomach, and I swallowed hard. Heath had always been a man of few words, and seeing him this tense, this focused, made me nervous.

"I don't want you to stay at Thornvale Manor just because Jasper asked you to," he continued, his voice steady. "I want you to stay because... because you truly want to."

The simplicity of his statement took me aback. I stared at him, lost for words. He shifted closer, his hand finding mine, fingers intertwining in a firm, reassuring grip.

"And I want you to stay because…" he paused, holding my eye, "because I have feelings for you, Jasmine."

His confession hung in the air as if the world had stopped spinning for a moment. I felt my heart pound against my chest, my breath hitching in my throat. A wave of emotions washed over me - surprise, joy, relief, but above all, an overwhelming sense of rightness. Confessing feelings that mirrored my own.

"Heath," I breathed out, squeezing his hand, "I have feelings for you too."

The words left my lips, soft and powerful and scented with velvety night and jasmine.

A relieved smile spread across his face, his eyes sparkling with an emotion that mirrored my own.

"So, will you stay, Jasmine?" he asked again.

His words echoed in my mind, igniting a warmth within me, a sense of... happiness. This was what I had been hoping for, even though I hadn't admitted it to myself until now. I looked into his eyes, saw the sincerity and hope reflected in them, and I knew my answer.

"Yes, Heath," I said, my voice filled with conviction. "I'll stay. With you."

Meeting his eyes, I smiled. His hand gently cupped my cheek, his thumb brushing my skin lightly, causing a trail of goosebumps to erupt across my skin. I found myself leaning into his touch, letting my eyes flutter and then close.

His lips met mine softly, hesitantly, as if seeking permission. I responded, my hand coming up to grasp his shirt, pulling him closer. His kiss deepened, his tongue exploring mine for what felt like a delightful eternity.

A sudden rustling from a nearby bush made us pull apart. We scanned the darkness, both of us breathless and flushed. He straightened, his eyes narrowing as he turned towards the source of the noise. I clutched his arm.

"Do you think... could it be a... a ghost?" I whispered. Thornvale Manor was old, and the rumours of it being haunted had circulated for as long as I could remember, so it wasn't entirely impossible to encounter a ghost, I figured.

Heath chuckled, the sound rich and warm in the quiet night. "I highly doubt that," he said, but his eyes stayed fixed on the bush.

"But what if—" I protested, only to be interrupted by a sudden yowl and a white blur shooting out from the foliage.

I jumped, but a moment later, laughter bubbled up from my chest. Out of the underbrush, a dishevelled and highly indignant Buttons, emerged. His tail was puffed up like a bottle brush, and he gave us a disgruntled look.

"Oh, it's just Buttons," I giggled, releasing Heath's arm to crouch down and coax the cat over. He pointedly ignored me, disappearing into the dark again.

I honestly still had my doubts that the cat wasn't simply a ghost. It would explain his sudden appearances in various random places.

But before I could ponder this issue further, Heath's lips were on mine again. He pressed his thumb underneath my chin, deepening our kiss; the other pressed down my lower back. My fingers trailed through his hair, dark and silky as the night. I have never been kissed like that: like the world would burn into ashes if we were to stop. His teeth were hard against my lips, clashing against mine, our bodies desperate to close the small gap that remained between us.

Suddenly, Heath pulled away from our kiss. He trailed his fingers down my cheek, his touch igniting my skin. The stars around me danced as I blinked a few times, my head dizzy, my body yearning for more.

"Jasmine," his voice was a low rumble, each syllable vibrating through me. "I've got to be honest with you. It's been a while since I first started fantasising about more than just our garden collaboration."

His bold statement left me blushing but also emboldened. I retorted, "Really now, Heath? I never pegged you as the type to mix business with pleasure."

He grinned, clearly delighted by my cheeky response. "I usually don't, but you, Jasmine Ackerley, you've got me breaking all my rules."

"Well, in that case, what did you have in mind?" I asked playfully.

"I have many things in mind, actually," he confessed, his eyes dropping to my lips before he continued, "But for the moment, I hope you're not too attached to these clothes."

Taken aback, I laughed, the air between us thick with tension. "And why would that be?" I asked, the challenge clear in my voice.

He leaned in closer, his breath warm against my ear. "Because I intend to take them off," he murmured, the promise in his voice making my heart flutter.

I raised a brow at him, leaning back to take in his face. "Quite confident, aren't we?" I teased, my heart pounding in my chest.

He leaned in again, his lips brushing mine as he whispered, "Very. I promise you... by the time I'm done with you, you'll be begging for more."

Heath Thornvale, of course, wasn't wrong.

Afterwards, long after midnight turned the sky the colour of ink, we lay down beneath the soft cotton sheets. Our clothes were scattered around the cosy bedroom, filled with the scent of musk and jasmine, the scent of the night that was full of fire. I was ready to beg him for more, my body pleasantly exhausted but still responding to his presence with the most delicious waves of desire deep in my lower belly. The hum of a quiet summer night outside the open window filled the room, complemented by the soft rustle of the nearby trees, and at least for a moment, I wanted to enjoy this sense of peace - the kind of contentment that only a true home can bring. A place where I could put down my roots so they could grow and bloom into something wonderful.

Home.

Was that what Thornvale Manor had become to me?

I rested my head on Heath's chest, his arm wrapped securely around me, our bare skin brushing against each other. He traced lazy circles on my shoulder, his fingers a comforting presence. The scent of him, earthy and masculine, was intoxicating, and I couldn't help but nuzzle closer to him.

In the sound of his heart beating, I found my answer.

Turning my eyes towards the open window, I observed the late summer moon hanging low in the star-studded sky, its glow casting a silver sheen over the garden. It would bloom again, I was sure - even now, I could see some of the flowers budding again despite being ravaged by the storm.

My heart swelled with a sense of accomplishment and happiness, and I turned to look back to Heath. His eyes were closed, a serene expression on his face. He looked so peaceful, so different from the man I had first met. We couldn't be sure about the manor's future, but we'd made a good start.

Curling myself tighter against him in the quaint little cottage, I felt happier than ever. And as I drifted off to sleep, my last thought was of how amazing it would be to wake up to another beautiful day in the place I now called home, in the arms of the man I loved.

The End

AUTHOR'S NOTE

Thank you for picking up my book – I hope you enjoyed it! I would appreciate if you could leave me a review on Amazon: this helps the new readers find my books.
And if you would like to find more about my upcoming books, you can find me on Instagram @aniawhiteley

Coming soon!

MIDNIGHTS OF
Memories

Sienna Thornvale's life has always been about the hustle - chasing deadlines, climbing the corporate ladder, and sealing the next big deal. But an unexpected career pause sends her on a detour to Thornvale Manor, her ancestral home. A December escape, filled with frosty mornings and festive nights with her siblings, seems harmless enough. But the snowstorm brings an unexpected guest: Carston Sorensen, once upon a time, Sienna's childhood sweetheart.

With each advent calendar door that opens, Sienna finds herself drawn into a whirlwind of old memories, rekindled feelings, and the magic of the holiday season. But Sienna doesn't have time for romance - and she sincerely believes that forced proximity with Carston will not affect that.

As the holiday spirit works its charm, frosty mornings and candlelit evenings stir old emotions and rekindle forgotten moments. With mistletoe hung in every corner and the scent of pine in the air, can Sienna keep her emotions under wraps?

Dive into a world of wintry wonder, where midnights bring the memories, secrets are unwrapped, and love might just find its way under the Christmas tree.

Printed in Great Britain
by Amazon